HOMECOMING?
AND OTHER STORIES

HOMECOMING?
AND OTHER STORIES

by

HAN SHAOGONG

translated by Martha Cheung

— An Authorized Collection —

A *RENDITIONS* Paperback

This collection first published 1992
Reprinted 1995

Renditions Paperbacks
are published by
The Research Centre for Translation
The Chinese University of Hong Kong

General Editors
Eva Hung   T.L. Tsim

Printed in Hong Kong

To My Parents

Contents

Introduction

Han Shaogong 韓少功 was born in Changsha, Hunan, in 1953. He was in junior middle school when the Cultural Revolution broke out in 1966 and was sent down to work in a rural commune. In 1969, he and a few friends volunteered to join another commune in an even remoter part of Hunan province. He spent three years there, living with a peasant household and working in the fields. In 1974, he was assigned to a cultural centre in a small provincial town and there he began to write short stories. In 1978, he returned to Changsha and went to the Hunan Normal University to read Chinese Literature. After graduation, he worked as an editor before becoming a professional writer. He now lives on Hainan Island with his wife and daughter. He has published five collections of short stories and novellas and has won literary prizes in both the People's Republic and Taiwan. Some of his early works have been translated into Russian and Japanese while the more recent ones have appeared in translation in English, French, and German. An Italian translation will also be published this year.

The works in this collection — two short stories and two novellas[1] — represent a crucial stage in Han's writing career.

---

[1]These works are collected in Han Shangong, *Youhuo* (*Lure*) (Changsha: Hunan wenyi chubanshe, 1986). The present translation is based on this Chinese edition.

Written between 1985-1986, these stories mark Han's development from a social-realist writer interested in depicting peasant life to an experimental writer spurred on by an active, almost obsessive, preoccupation with history, with Time past and Time present, with tradition, and, above all, with culture. The change is primarily one of perception. If in his pre-1985 works Han perceived the relation between literature and reality as essentially mimetic, with literature functioning as a mirror reflection of reality, then in his post-1985 works, he perceives the same relationship as a dialogic one, with literature functioning as a mediator of reality, shaping and moulding it into something that can be examined from different angles.

One integral part of reality which Han looks at is the impact of the Cultural Revolution on the Chinese people, which is also the concern of many other Chinese writers. But Han's works are distinctly different from the "wound literature" which appeared in the years immediately after the Cultural Revolution and which expresses, in intensely emotional, often unbearably bitter, terms, the painful experience which the writers had gone through during those ten difficult years. The Cultural Revolution casts a long dark shadow in Han's works, but there is no unleashing of raw emotion, and no impatient dismissal. The experience of that traumatic event is turned into material for thought, and his fiction becomes a timely inquiry into what there is in Chinese culture that permitted such an event to take place.

The first two stories in this collection, "Homecoming?" and "The Blue Bottle-cap", can be read together as an attempt to reveal, delineate, and examine the cataclysmal changes wrought in human consciousness by the Cultural Revolution. But Han's treatment of this subject is subtle. The Cultural Revolution figures only in the background, not as the immediate setting of the story. And the political dimension is implicit rather than overtly present. "Homecoming?" tells the story of Huang Zhixian, an educated youth who, on a trip to a remote mountain village, is mistaken by the peasants of a village he happens to pass through for a certain "Glasses Ma". He does not clarify this mistake, and thus gets himself involved in a nightmarish experience — he loses his sense of self, is inexplicably overwhelmed by uneasy feelings of guilt and wrongdoing, and finally has to run away from the village like a fugitive. By setting the story in a time and place that has only a tenuous link with the Cultural Revolution, Han gives it a surreal quality, allowing it to be read on many levels. His protagonist's experience will certainly stir up deep emotional reverberations in his Mainland readers, for it is an experience which countless people must have gone through during the Cultural Revolution — being accused, often for no reason whatsoever, of having committed sins and crimes of which they were innocent. And, in this sense, the story can be taken as a denunciation of the debilitating effects of the Cultural Revolution on the human psyche.

Significantly, however, Huang Zhixian's plight is largely one of his own making. At every stage in this eerie drama of mistaken identity, Huang could have extricated himself from the situation but he never did. Why? The question cries out to be answered but it is not, thus provoking yet another question. Is the author asking his readers to put the blame on his protagonist? By implication, is the author urging his readers to look at the Cultural Revolution from an angle wider than the purely denunciatory?

From such an angle, the scenario emerges that *perhaps* the Cultural Revolution occurred and developed into such a catastrophic event because people allowed it to happen. Because, when they were accused of being someone other than themselves, they had *perhaps* not fought hard enough to defend their sense of who they are. And because there is *perhaps* something in Chinese culture which discourages the emergence of a fully developed sense of identity and thus encourages abject submission.

"Perhaps" is the key word here, for while there are hints in the story which suggest that the protagonist is responsible for his own

plight, there is no explicit finger-pointing. Han's use of the protagonist as also the first-person narrator of the story has precluded that.
Likewise, there is no clear indication as to the exact factors in
Chinese culture that hamper a fully developed sense of self. The
last line of the story, in which the protagonist remarks, "I'm tired,
I'll never be able to get away from that gigantic I", carries a
thought-provoking metaphor. One wonders whether or not the
"gigantic I" refers to the "collective self" before which the individual
"I" has been taught, and is expected, to bow. One wonders whether
or not it is the dominance of the collective self in the traditional
Confucian ethical system that has discouraged the individual from
taking seriously the question "who am I?", or simply taking the
question as one of positioning — I am a Chinese, I am a member
of the Communist Party, I am a member of my clan, etc.

One wonders, but finds no answer in the story. This is why the
story stirred up so much discussion when it was first published in
China. Readers and critics alike saw it as a major departure from
the moralistic, didactic, and propaganda modes of writing that
have for decades dominated the Chinese literary scene. They
responded to the dream-like mixture of past and present in the
story, to the unnerving sense of guilt that envelops the narrative.
Above all, they responded to the spirit of inquiry which permeates
the story. For few Chinese readers could emerge from the experience of reading this story without asking themselves, willingly or
unwillingly, some of these questions: Who am "I"?, What am "I"?,
When I say "I", what do I mean? Who am I referring to? What am I
identifying myself with? How can I "get away from that gigantic I"?
How do I disentangle myself from the "not-I" which others may
impose on me?

The same spirit of inquiry, as distinguished from that of inves-
tigation, informs "The Blue Bottle-cap". Again, the work explores
the question of guilt and responsibility. It is made up of two stories.
The inner story is about how Chen Mengtao, a person who has been

sent to work in a labour camp (the Cultural Revolution is again implicitly present) buckles under the pressure and goes mad, "calmly and amicably". The outer story is about how the "I" narrator meets this mad man and learns about his story, and about the impact of such a story on him. Like "Homecoming?", "Bottle-cap" also presents its readers with different possibilities of reading. We can say that the writer, by framing the story of Chen, is employing a detached, totally unemotional narrative method to bring out the mental and psychological pressure inflicted on man by the cruel reality of a period in history and the story is therefore a powerful, if subdued, condemnation of the Cultural Revolution. We can also say that Chen's story, like "Homecoming?", is really about responsibility, about how Chen, because of his own weaknesses, loses his mind. Or we can say that the story is about both: while history is responsible for an individual's fate, the individual, too, has to be responsible for his own fate; the two are inextricably linked and the apportioning of blame is never a simple matter.

If we also take the outer story into consideration, we may come up with yet another interpretation. The outer story is not just a framing device but an uncanny re-enactment of the inner story. Chen, we are told, has gone mad "calmly and amiably" and, "apart from his fixation with bottle-caps", he seems "quite normal". Could it not also be said that the last few paragraphs of "Bottle-cap", which bring the outer story to an end, are really about how the "I" narrator goes mad, calmly and amiably? Doesn't his fixation with the bottle-cap bear a striking similarity to Chen's fixation?

If this be the case, then "Bottle-cap", like "Homecoming?" expresses responses to the Cultural Revolution that transcend the purely emotive. Anger and condemnation are evoked in order to be purged. The story takes up the question of guilt — inexplicable guilt — and attempts to explain it, in a way that is perhaps best illumined by these words in E. M. Forster's *A Passage to India*: "... nothing can be performed in isolation. All perform a good action, when one is performed, and when an evil action is performed, all perform it".[2]

Han, in this story, looks at the question of guilt in a similar manner. Before evil, no one can remain unmoved. Even if you are not the wrongdoer, you would, before you know it, have assumed the responsibility yourself and felt the burden somehow. No one is putting the blame on you, but this "assumption of responsibility" occurs naturally. It is not human weakness; it is human nature. The inner story is about how Chen realizes, if only dimly and murkily, that the death of an inmate in the labour camp is not just the death of one person, but a manifestation of evil. It shows how the "assumption of responsibility" occurs, how the sense of inexplicable guilt drives Chen to madness. Likewise, the outer story is about how the "I" narrator realizes, if only dimly and murkily, that the story of Chen is not simply an after-dinner story to be dismissed as soon as it is told; rather, it is also a manifestation of evil. He, too, feels suddenly overwhelmed by an inexplicable sense of guilt. He, too, comes to an end eerily similar to Chen's.

"After such knowledge, what forgiveness?" T. S. Eliot's line sums up the effect this discovery has on the reader. Having come to the knowledge that no one can disclaim responsibility for the horrors of history, forgiveness does seem beside the point. Such a knowledge may not help to heal the scars of history, but it does make them more bearable. If "Homecoming?" dramatizes for us a vision of history as a "nightmare from which one could never awake", then "Bottle-cap" marks the writer's effort to shake off that nightmare by coming to terms with history. "Homecoming?" explores what, in Han's words, are the "cultural factors which constrain man", "Bottle-cap" attempts to provide a more balanced view by showing that there is yet something in culture that can help to

[2] E. M. Forster, *A Passage to India* (Penguin 1985), p. 169.

liberate man. Han has obviously been inspired by anecdotes about the *Chan* patriarchs, who respond to their followers' questions with answers that stimulate thinking, so that when truth dawns on the listener, it comes like an intuitive insight, a sudden epiphany.[3] "Bottle-cap" is a moving plea for a more enlightened view of history.

But the critical gaze of Han Shaogong is fastened not only on the past, on history, but also on the present, on history as it evolves in China. He is acutely conscious that there is now in China a spiritual vacuum — of the sort best summed up in W. B. Yeats' line, "the old is dead, the new is yet to be born". What is dead or lost forever is people's capacity for total and unconditional belief — whether it be in Marxism, or Communism, or Maoism, or in traditional Confucian values and ideals. The capacity and the yearning for belief are still there, but a new focus is yet to be found. There are many competing forces vying to fill that vacuum, many powerful hands struggling to steer the course of history. Han's "Pa Pa Pa" and "Woman Woman Woman" capture this process and actually participate in it.

"Pa Pa Pa" looks at history at the same time as it looks at history in the making. The story takes place in the by now familiar landscape of Han's works — a remote mountain village that seems to exist outside time and totally untouched by the prevailing social changes. It is about the decline in fortunes of a village clan, a saga that also bears no ostensible relation to the immediate present or

---

[3] *Chan* is a Chinese school of Mahayana Buddhism founded in the 6th century AD by the Indian teacher Bodhidharma. It emphasizes meditation and higher contemplation as the way to enlightenment. It is the Chinese equivalent of the Japanese *Zen* or the Indian *Dhyana*. Han Shaogong, at the end of another story in this collection, "Woman Woman Woman", has incorporated into the narrative one anecdote about the teachings of the *Chan* patriarchs. This is how it goes: a monk asks a *Chan* patriarch what is the true self of a Buddhist follower, the patriarch, instead of replying, asks the monk, "Have you eaten?", when the monk has said yes, the patriarch says, "Then go and wash the bowl."

to any definite period in history. And yet, precisely because the story seems so timeless, it acquires an enigmatic quality the significance of which must be uncovered. Mainland Chinese critics have been quick to rise to the challenge. Some see it as a satiric piece of work written in the tradition best represented by Lu Xun, with its description of barbaric rituals, totem worship, feuds between village clans and other primitive practices being a merciless exposure of the forces that are stalling the pace of modernization in China: ignorance, narrow-mindedness, superstition, provincialism, conservatism, complacency. Some regard the story as a cultural critique, a delineation of the deep structure of Chinese culture that is manifested in the habits, customs, traditions, beliefs, rituals, songs, legends, language and behaviour of the people that figure in the story. Some read it as a kind of mood poem, the dominant mood being nostalgia, as the writer seems to be trying to preserve in writing a way of life that is on the verge of extinction. Yet others dismiss it as mere writer's indulgence in his taste for the exotic, the story's folksy style and vivid portrayal of remote mountain life being no more than the writer's effort to give his work a sense of novelty, at best a *tour de force*, a Chinese version of magic realism, but more probably a fancy piece that will not stand the test of time.

"Pa Pa Pa" does lend itself to all these readings. And one could perhaps add that the story also comes over as a powerful fable with a severe warning about the fate of China. Certainly, the condition of the village and its inhabitants can be taken as a symbolic representation of the condition of the country and its people: backward and inward-looking, bogged down by the weight of tradition and the former glory of its civilization. What is more, since attempts at reforms are clearly ineffectual, the place, and by implication, the country, is in grave danger of coming to a sad end so that the young and the strong will have to leave, and only the stupid and the idiotic will survive. For Young Bing, the idiot whose speech is limited to two expressions, "Papa" and "F___ Mama", does survive.

A severe warning indeed. Depressing, too. But the story, from whichever angle it is looked at, is as much about defeat as it is about triumph — the triumph of the human spirit. The people are defeated, but they accept it with dignity and fortitude. If there is no grandeur in defeat, there is no abject misery either. The overall mood is heavy, but not unbearably so. Idiocy and stupidity do survive, and that is a grave indictment. But the story, with its constant references to the creation myth and the tales of survival and migration in Chinese mythology, sets defeat and decline against a long perspective — to be measured not in terms of decades, or even centuries, but of millennia — so that what emerges is a sense of the life energy and the amazing resilience of the Chinese race.

Like "Pa Pa Pa", "Woman Woman Woman" provides colourful details about life in a remote mountain village. The scope of this piece, however, is broader as Han also depicts life in the city, putting the two in sharp contrast. Moreover, the story is set in China in the 1980s, though the narrative still moves freely between the present and the past, and crosses and re-crosses the boundary line between the real and the unreal. The story is about the "I" narrator's relationship with three women — his aunt, Aunt Yao; her sworn sister, Aunnt Zhen; and Lao Hei, Aunt Yao's goddaughter. Aunt Yao is a factory worker who leads an extremely frugal life, frugal to the point of self-denial, but she has generously helped the narrator and his family through their most difficult times during the Cultural Revolution. She is simple-minded, and yet her throw-away remarks, never taken seriously by anyone, often contain profound wisdom. Aunt Zhen lives in the country and takes up the responsibility of looking after Aunt Yao after she has had a stroke and has become an impossible burden to the narrator and his family. It is a punishing job, but she accepts it with resignation, saying that it is the will of heaven. In stark contrast to these two women, Lao Hei is a westernized young woman who leads a wild, self-indulgent life, completely unfettered by the manners and morals of the times. And yet her extreme individualism often makes the narrator uneasily aware of the inadequacy of his own values and beliefs. The three women have such different outlooks on life and such contrasting values that they are obviously meant to be taken as signifiers in a model — any interpretive model. And the narrator's mixed and conflicting responses towards them — guilty resentment, irrepressible annoyance, grudging appreciation — highlight at once the spiritual muddle in present day China, particularly among the intellectuals, as well as an individual's struggle to find a way out of such a situation.

In many ways, "Woman Woman Woman" is a summation of Han's works, not only in the sense that questions of guilt, responsibility and selfhood are further explored, but also in the sense that these questions are resolved, if not on an intellectual level, at least on an emotional level. It is also a summation in the sense that the work not only portrays history and history in the making, culture and culture in ferment, but also releases the writer's deepest feelings towards his culture and his country's past.

Indeed, it is as if the three earlier works all lead up to this one; as if the writer's feelings, subdued and held under control in the earlier pieces, could no longer be suppressed and must be given an outlet, must be allowed to burst.

And burst they did. Like fierce torrents, like a deluge, like an earthquake — images which figure prominently in the story. They come, not with a whimper but with a bang — in a single paragraph that will almost certainly assume its rightful place in literature as a unique example of how emotions could be handled.

This is the paragraph which describes the earthquake that hits the village while Aunt Yao's burial ceremony is in progress but which in fact is also a description of the emotional turmoil that shakes the protagonist and the author. The range of emotions expressed is astonishing. There is grief, bereavement and pain.

There is puzzle and bewilderment about the meaning of life and death, anxiety to know the significance of time, wonder at the mystery of the universe, fascination with the history of Chinese civilization and that of its people, gratitude for having been born and bred in such a country, and deep concern about its future. References and allusions are used in a wild medley of snatches of history and fragments of culture. Familiar quotations and sayings taken from classical Chinese poetry and from religious and philosophical texts are juxtaposed to produce the effect of an echo chamber, in which is heard the rich and diverse voices of civilization speaking in unison. The sentences often end in the form of a question or they are punctuated with questions, so that the whole passage is shot through and through with an urgent sense of yearning — the yearning for enlightenment. Images come in clusters to call up a vision of heaven in all its glory and splendour, and simultaneously a vision of earth shaking, crumbling, in ruins, in desolation. Punctuation gives way to a rhythmic eruption of feelings in all their feverish intensity.

It is amazing how much the writer is able to pack into this single paragraph, and how complex the story is. The range, depth, and intensity of feeling the story expresses, the richness of its texture, the poetry, verve, and energy of its writing, the breadth and scope of its subject matter, and the enormous room it provides for interpretive exploration all make it the finest and most impressive work Han Shaogong has produced to date. It is possibly also one of the finest and most impressive fictional works produced in Mainland China in the post-Cultural Revolution era.

Han Shaogong is certainly one of the most prominent writers in Mainland China today, prominent because his works often set a new trend for other writers to follow. In 1985, when a lot of intellectuals and writers were turning their backs on traditional Chinese culture and looking for Western literary models, Han raised a question which sparked off a heated debate: Where should a Chinese writer look for sustenance? Han warned against a total rejection of traditional culture, and insisted that there were elements in Chinese civilization and culture that are astonishingly beautiful and can be used to reinvigorate China's ailing literary scene. The four stories collected here are eloquent testimony of his belief and the fruits of his effort. There is an abundance of stock images and conventional symbols, of allusions and references to familiar philosophical and religious texts, as well as to stories drawn from classical Chinese mythology, but there is nothing hackneyed or derivative about their usage. Instead, there is an exciting sense of many familiar voices speaking, or rather singing, together. And what this chorus produces is a splendid and magnificent song — a beautiful hymn of praise to the history, the culture, and the people that have made China what it is.

A hymn of praise — that's what Han Shaogong's works are. What is more, it is a hymn that at times reaches a note of ecstasy, i.e., of great pleasure derived from great pain, of intense joy rising from intense sorrow. For there is no denying that his stories are steeped in pain and sorrow, in decrepitude too, and suffering.

But this is perhaps why Han's works will appeal not only to Chinese readers but also to readers outside China. The ecstasy of the writing is contagious and the reader will come away from the experience knowing that they have made the acquaintance of a writer who feels deeply for his people, his country, and his culture, and who is able to see its weaknesses and strengths with clear-sightedness, compassion, and, above all, with love. Yes, love — in the sublime sense of the word.

I would like to thank Han Shaogong for giving me permission to translate these stories and for being so helpful and patient in answering my questions. I would also like to thank the editors of *Renditions*, Chu Chiyu, Harriet Clompus, Janice Wickeri and Eva Hung, for having gone over the drafts of this translation with meticulous care and for their valuable suggestions. Cheng Yang-ping and Jamila Ismail have read the manuscript and their comments and criticisms have helped me come to a fresh appreciation of the demands of translation. Last but not the least, I would like to acknowledge a special debt of gratitude to Jane Lai, without whose help, support, encouragement and inspiration this translation would not have been possible.

Martha Cheung
January 1992

who are
born old?
perhaps read
as a poem

Homecoming?

People have often observed that, sometimes, when they visit a place for the first time, they find it familiar, yet they don't know why. This was what I felt now.

I was walking. Much of the dirt track had been washed out by water running down the slope, leaving jagged ridges of earth and mounds of pebbles, like a body stripped of skin and flesh, with sticks of dry bone and lumps of shrivelled innards fully exposed. There were a few rotting bamboos and a frayed length of the curb-rope of some buffalo or cow — a sign that a village would soon come into view. There were also some dark motionless shadows in the small pond beside the track. They looked like rocks at first glance, but a closer look showed them to be calves' heads, with eyes that were staring furtively at me. Wrinkled and bearded, these calves were born old, they had inherited old age at birth. Beyond the banana grove ahead loomed a square blockhouse, with blank staring gun embrasures, and dark walls that looked as if they had been charred by smoke and fire, as if they were the coagulation of many dark nights. I had heard that bandits had been rife in these parts in the past. If they weren't put down, there would be nobody on the land in ten years' time — so it was said. No wonder every village had its own blockhouse, and the houses of the mountain folk were never spread out but huddled together, sturdy, with mean little windows set high up to make it difficult for thieves to climb in.

All this looked so familiar and yet so strange. It was like looking at a written character: the harder you look at it, the more it looks like a character you know, and yet it doesn't look like the character you know. Damn! Had I been here before? Let me guess: follow the flagstone path, go round the banana grove and turn left at the oil-press, and perhaps I'd see an old tree behind the blockhouse, a ginkgo or a camphor, struck dead by lightning.

A little later, my guess was proved correct. Down to the hollow in the tree trunk, and, in front of it, two boys at play burning grass.

I ventured another guess: behind the tree, a low cow-shed perhaps, several heaps of cow-dung at the entrance, and a rusty plough or a harrow under the eaves. I walked over, and there they were, clear as day. Even the granite mortar and the pestle lying aslant, even the sand and the few fallen leaves in the mortar seemed vaguely familiar!

Of course, there was no muddy water in the mortar in my imagination. But come to think of it, it had been raining; the water must have dripped from the eaves. At this, a chill rose from my heels and crept all the way up to my neck.

No, I couldn't have been here before. Definitely not. I'd never had meningitis, never gone mad, and my mind was still in good shape. Had I seen this place in a film then? Heard it mentioned by friends, perhaps? Or dreamt about it ...? I searched my memory frantically.

The even more puzzling thing was, the mountain folk all seemed to know me. Just now, when I was cautiously picking my way among the boulders in the stream, my trouser legs rolled up, a man carrying on his shoulder two young trees tied into the shape of an "A" came towards me from upstream. Seeing how precariously I was balancing myself on the rocks, he threw me a dry branch pulled from a melon shed by the roadside and, much to my surprise, gave me a big grin, showing his yellow teeth.

"You're back?"

"Yes, I'm back ...."

"Must have been over ten years?"

"Ten years ...."

"Go and take a rest in my place. Sangui is ploughing the seedling beds in front of the house."

Where was his house? Who was Sangui? I was bewildered.

I went up a gentle slope. An expanse of eaves and tiled roofs and a doorway rose up before me.

I saw in the distance a few figures thrashing something on the ground. As I went up to them, I could hear the rhythmic clacking of their flails — a few loud clacks, then a softer one. They were all barefoot and had close-cropped hair, their faces were glazed with jagged trickles of brown sweat. As they moved about, patches of sweat on their cheeks gleamed in the sun. Their short jackets hung loose on their bodies, exposing the smooth skin on their bellies, and their navels. Their trousers also hung low on their hips. It was not until I saw one of them move towards a cradle and start breast-feeding a baby and then noticed the ear-rings they all had on that I realized they were women. One of them stared at me in amazement.

"Isn't this Ma ..."

"Glasses Ma." Another reminded her. They all giggled, amused by the name.

"My name is not Ma. I'm Huang ..."

"Changed your name?"

"No."

"Still such a tease? Where did you come from?"

"From the town, of course."

"A rare visitor! Where's sister Liang?"

"Which sister Liang?"

"Your wife. Isn't she called Liang?"

"No. My wife is called Yang."

"Did I remember it wrong? No, I can't be wrong. In those days she even told me her surname was the same as my family's. My family is from Sanjiangkou, Liangjiashe, you know that."

What did I know? Besides, what had that Liang, whatever her name, got to do with me? It seemed as if I'd wanted to go and find her, and ended up here somehow. I'd no idea how I got here.

The woman threw down the flail and showed me to her house. The threshold was high and solid. Innumerable people, young and old, must have trodden on it and sat on it to wear down that depression in the middle. The grain of the wood spread out on the threshold like yellow moonbeams, a fossil of yellow moonbeams. Kids had to crawl over it, grown-ups had to turn their bodies at an angle and lift their legs high before they could bring themselves in through the doorway. It was dark inside, you couldn't see a thing. Only a thin ray of light managed to creep in through the tiny high window, slicing open the damp darkness. The place smelled of chicken droppings and swill. It took a while for my eyes to adjust, to make out the walls and beams that were covered with ashes and soot, and the outline of an equally sooty hanging basket of some sort. I sat on a wood block, mildly surprised that there were no chairs, only benches and wood blocks. The women, young and old, packed the doorway, gibbering and jabbering. The one who was breast-feeding her baby was not at all inhibited by my presence. She pulled out her other long heavy breast and gave suck to her baby, the nipple of the one she had just removed from the baby's mouth still dripping milk, and she smiled at me. They were saying some strange things ... "Young Qin ..." "No, not Young Qin." "No?" "It's Young Ling." "Oh yes. Is Young Ling still teaching?" "Why doesn't she come and visit us?" "Have you all gone back to Changsha?" "Do you live in the city or the country?" "Have you got any kids?" "One or two?" "Has Young Luo got any kids?" "One or two?" "Has Chen Zhihua got any kids?" "One or two?" "What about Bearhead? Has he found himself a wife?" "Does he have kids? One or two?" ....

It was obvious that they had mistaken me for a certain 'Glasses Ma' who knew people by the name of Young Ling and Bearhead and the like. Perhaps that chap looked very much like me. Perhaps he, too, hid behind his glasses looking at people.

But who was he? And did I need to worry about that? The women's smiling faces told me there was no need to worry about food and shelter for today. Thank heavens! Let them take me for this Ma what's-his-name. I could easily handle their "One or two?" questions, surprise them a little or make them nod their heads in sympathy now and then. No sweat really.

The woman from Liangjiashe brought in a tray with four large bowls of sweet tea. I learnt later that this meant "peace all the year round", the four bowls standing for the four seasons. The rim of the bowl was dark and grimy, and I drank without touching it with my lips. But the tea was good and tasted of fried sesame and glutinous rice. She picked up from the floor two dirty garments belonging to her children, put them in a wooden tub, and carried it into the inner room. And so her sentence was cut into two: "We haven't had news of you for a long time, Old Shuigen said ... (it was quite a while before she emerged from the room) ... you were thrown into jail soon after you left us?"

I was so shocked I nearly scalded my hand with the tea. "No, I wasn't. What jail?"

"Old Shuigen doesn't know a thing then. What rubbish he talked! My poor father-in-law was in a terrible flap. He burnt lots of incense sticks for you." She covered her mouth in a fit of giggles, "Oh! I'm going to die laughing."

The women all burst out laughing. The one with a spread of yellow teeth added, "He even went to Yang's Hill to pray for you to the Buddha."

Rotten luck! Incense sticks and the Buddha! Well, maybe that chap Ma really had fallen into the hands of some evil spirit and was doomed to end up in jail. And here I was, sipping tea in his place, laughing like an idiot.

The woman served me another bowl of sweet tea, her free hand holding the wrist of the one carrying the bowl, as she had done before. Part of the local etiquette, I suppose. But I hadn't yet finished the first bowl. There wasn't much tea left, but the sesame and the rice were still sitting at the bottom of the bowl, and I had no idea how to eat them politely. "He missed you, he said you were kind and just, and you had a good heart. He wore your padded jacket for many winters. When he died, I turned it into a pair of trousers for our little Man ...."

I wanted to talk about the weather.

The room suddenly grew dark. I turned round and saw a dark shadow almost completely blocking the doorway. It was a man naked to the waist, his bulging muscles hard and angular like rock, not smooth and curved. He was carrying something which looked in silhouette like a buffalo's head. The shadow loomed over me. Before I could see the face clearly, he dropped what he was carrying with a loud thud, and I felt the file-like surface of two enormous palms rubbing my hands.

"It's Comrade Ma! Well, well, well ...."

I wasn't a caterpillar, why was I scared stiff?

He turned towards the brazier and the flames lit up the side of his face. I saw a big grin, a black gaping mouth, and arms sporting green tattoos.

"Comrade Ma, when did you arrive?"

I wanted to say that my name wasn't Ma but Huang, Huang Zhixian. And I hadn't come to revisit this place or to explore it out of a sense of adventure.

"Do you know me? (Does he mean 'recognize'? Or 'remember'?) I was in Spiral Hill building roads the year you left.

I'm Ai Ba."

"Ai Ba. Yes, yes. I know you." What a contemptible answer. "You were the team leader then."

"No, not the team leader, I recorded work points. And do you still know my wife?"

"Yes, yes. I do. She was good at making sweet tea."

"I went to chase meat with you once, do you still know? ('to chase meat', does it mean 'hunting'?) I wanted to make some offerings to the mountain gods, but you called ('said'?) I was superstitious. And what happened? You stumbled into some poisonous grass and got nasty boils all over your body. You also came upon a muntjac deer. It ran between your legs, but you missed it ...."

"Yes. Yes, I missed it, by an inch. My eyes aren't very good."

The black gaping mouth exploded into laughter. The women stood up lazily and, swaying their heavy hips, left the room. The man who called himself Ai Ba took out a bottle gourd, poured the drink into two large bowls and invited me to drink. The wine looked murky. It was sweet, but it also had a bitter, burning taste. I was told it contained medicinal herbs and tiger bonnes. He turned down my offer of a cigarette, and rolled his own with a bit of newspaper. He drew a deep puff and the paper burst into a bright flame. He wasn't at all worried, he didn't even look at it. I watched him anxiously, and it was a while before he puffed out the flame in one leisurely breath, the cigarette still intact.

"We have good times now, plenty of meat and plenty to drink. At the Spring Festival, every household slaughtered a cow to celebrate." He wiped his mouth, "That year when every village had to be run on the Dazhai[1] model, nobody got paid anything. You know all about that, of course."

---

[1] A production brigade in Xiyang County, Shanxi Province, the pace-setter for agriculture in China.

"Yes, yes I do." But I wanted to talk about the good times.

"Have you watched Delong? He's now our chief. He went to Zhuomei Bridge to plant trees yesterday. Mayhap he'll come back, mayhap he won't, and then mayhap he would." Then he started to talk about things and people that puzzled and bewildered me: so-and-so had built a new house, sixteen feet high; so-and-so too, it was eighteen feet high; so-and-so was about to build one, also eighteen feet high; and so-and-so was laying the foundations, mayhap it'd be sixteen feet high, mayhap eighteen. I listened nervously, trying to work out the implications his words might have. I found the vocabulary used by the people here somewhat peculiar: "see" became "watch", "quiet" became "clean". Then there was the word "gather" — did it mean "rise"? Or did it mean "stand"?

I felt a bit tipsy and made a show of enthusiasm at every mention of the figures — sixteen feet, eighteen feet.

"You haven't forgotten us in the mountain then. You've come back to watch how we're doing." He took another pull at his cigarette, and for a moment or two the bright flame again drove me to distraction. "You know, I've kept the books you gave out when you were a teacher here." He went rat-a-tat up the stairs and a long time elapsed before he came down again, cobwebs in his hair, beating the dust off a few yellow tattered sheets of paper. It was a mimeographed booklet with the front and back cover missing, a sort of primer probably, and smelt of damp and tung oil. It contained what looked like night-school songs, a miscellany of agricultural terms, the characters '1911 Revolution', Marx's essays on the peasants' movement, and a map. The printing was crude, the characters were huge and the pages stained with ink blots. I didn't think there was anything great about these characters, I knew how to write them myself.

"You were really down on your luck then. You looked quite starved, just a pair of eyes in your gaunt face. But you still came here to teach."

"Oh! It was nothing. Nothing!"

"It was the last month of the lunar year. Heavy snow, freezing cold."

"That's right. So cold my nose nearly froze off."

"And we still had to go and work in the fields, using pine torches to light our way."

"Ah, pine torches."

All of a sudden, his manner grew mysterious. The two bright patches on his cheeks and the cluster of drinker's spots drew close to my face. "Tell me, did you kill Shortie Yang?"

What Shortie Yang? My skull suddenly contracted, my mouth and jaws went stiff, and I shook my head vehemently. My name simply wasn't Ma, and I'd never met anyone called Shortie Yang. Why did I have to get sucked into a criminal case?

"They all said you killed him. Served him right. That slimy two-headed snake!" He snarled. But, seeing me shake my head, he stared at me, incredulous, disappointed.

"Can I have another drink?" I tried to change the topic.

"Sure, sure. Help yourself."

"There are mosquitoes here."

"Yes. They pick on strangers. Shall I burn some straw?"

He lit some straw. More people had arrived in groups to see me and were greeting me with the usual polite questions about my health and my family. The men lit the cigarettes I offered them and went to sit by the door or by the wall, puffing away noisily, smiling but saying little. Now and then they exchanged a few remarks about me among themselves. Some said I had grown fat, others said I had lost weight; some said I had aged, others said I still looked "young-faced" and it had to do with the rich food I ate in the city. When they finished smoking, they took their leave with a smile, saying that they had to fell some trees or to apply manure on their fields. A few kids had gathered round me, they stared hard at my glasses for a while and then dashed off into hiding, screaming in an ecstasy of fear and excitement, "There are little devils inside! Little devils!" A young woman was standing by the door chewing a blade of grass and watching me with an absorbed expression, her eyes glistening as if with tears, I had no idea why. Feeling awkward and uneasy, I turned and fixed my eyes politely on Ai Ba.

I had been through scenes like this already. Just now when I went to take a look at their opium fields, I met a middle-aged woman. She looked terrified as soon as she saw me, the colour draining from her face like a lamp suddenly going dim, and she quickly pulled up the back straps of her shoes, lowered her head and changed direction to avoid me, I didn't know why.

Ai Ba said I ought to pay a visit to Third Grandpa. Actually, Third Grandpa had passed away. They said he had died from a snake-bite not long ago. But his name still cropped up in conversation, and his desolate little house still stood beside the brick-kiln. Flanked by two tung trees, the house was leaning precariously to one side and looked as though it would collapse at any moment. Around the house there were weeds waist-high. They were creeping up the front steps with sinister determination, their tongue-like blades quivering, waiting to swallow up the little house as if they were about to devour the remaining bones of a clan. The padlocked wooden door was full of black holes bored by worms. I wondered whether the house would have become so dilapidated if its master had been alive. Could it be that the man was the soul of the house and when the soul was gone, the body would rot in no time? A rusty lantern lay overturned in the grass, its surface dotted with white bird-droppings. Close to it stood a broken earthenware jar. When you touched it, mosquitoes swarmed out buzzing. Ai Ba told me that this jar was used for pickling vegetables and that in those days I often came here for Third Grandpa's pickled cucumber. (Did I?) The plaster on the walls had flaked off, leaving only the barest outline of a few large characters, "Eyes on the world". Ai Ba said I had painted them on. (Had I?) He picked a bunch of herbs and studied the birds' nests on the tree. I peered at the inside of the house through the window and saw a basket half full of lime standing in one corner, and what looked like a large round tray. A closer look told me it was an iron barbell disc, badly rusted. I was amazed — how could an unusual piece of sports equipment like that have found its way into the heart of the mountain? How did it get here?

But there was probably no need to ask Ai Ba — I'd given it to Third Grandpa as a present. Had I? And I'd given it to him so he could make it into a hoe or a harrow, and he never did. Was that right?

Someone up the slope was calling his cow, "Wuma — Wuma —." And the faint tinkle of cow bells came from the woods on the other side. They had an unusual way of calling cows here. It sounded like a sad desolate call for mamma. Perhaps the walls of the block-house had turned black because of these dismal wailings.

An old woman was coming down the hill, a small bundle of firewood on her back. She was bent almost double and with every step, her hoe-like protruding chin dipped as if it was digging at the ground. She looked up at me, her cloudy pupils pressed hard against her upper eyelids, and gave me a long stare that seemed to go right through me to the tung trees behind. There was no expression on her face, just lines and wrinkles so deep I was stunned. She glanced at Third Grandpa's little house and then turned round to look at the old tree at the entrance to the village. "The tree has died too," she mumbled to herself all of a sudden. Then, step by step, she trundled off, dipping her chin, and the thin silvery strands on her head were pressed down by the wind, pressed down by the wind.

I was now sure I'd never been here before. And I couldn't figure out the meaning of the old woman's remark — it was unfathomable, like a deep dark pool.

The evening meal was a grand feast. Chunks of beef and pork

the size of a palm were brought out in a large bowl extended at the
rim with straw hoops. The meat, underdone and greasy, was stacked
up high in the bowl, one piece on top of another, like a pile of bricks
in a kiln. People must have eaten like this for thousands of years.
Only the men could sit round the table. One of the guests did not
turn up but the host put a piece of rough straw paper at the empty
place and served food to the absent guest all the same. During the
meal I asked about their fragrant rice but they refused to talk about
the price, insisting I should take some as a present. As for the opium,
they had had a good yield this year but the national pharmaceutical
agency had a monopoly on it. At this, I decided not to pursue the
matter further.

"Shortie Yang had it coming to him." Ai Ba slurped a spoonful
of soup, put the spoon back at its sticky place on the table and
turned his eyes to the meat bowl again, tapping the table with his
chopsticks. "Fat-arsed, plump-pawed, he couldn't do a thing. And
he wanted to build a house. The bloody schemer!"

"Damn right you are! And who hasn't been tied up by that
bloody rope of his? See, I've still got two scars on my wrists. That
fucking son-of-a-bitch."

"How did he die? Did he really bump into a blood-sucking
demon and fall over a cliff?"

"You can be mean and ruthless, but you can't beat Fate. And
yet some people are never content. They want more than heaven
gives them. Hongsheng over at Xia's Bay is like that too."

"Shortie even ate rats. It's diabolical!"

"Absolutely! Never heard anything like it in my life!"

"Rotten luck for Bearhead too! Shortie slapped him hard on
the face twice. Bags of dye they were, I saw them with my own eyes.
Wasn't even good enough for dying cloth, only good for painting
clay buddhas. But Shortie insisted it was gunpowder."

"Well, it had something to do with Bearhead's class background
too."

I plucked up my courage and interposed, "Did the higher-ups send someone to investigate?"

Ai Ba said, chewing a piece of fat noisily, "They did. They fucking did! They even tried to question me, but I slipped away in time, saying that I'd to go and look for a hen that had gone missing .... Hey, Comrade Ma, you haven't touched your drink! Come, come, help yourself to more meat."

My throat tightened as he thrust another chunk of meat on me. I had to make like I was going to get some more rice and, as soon as I was in the shadow, I threw the meat to a dog squeezing past my legs.

After dinner, they insisted on letting me take a bath. I wondered whether it was a local custom, and warned myself not to behave like a new-comer. There was no bath-tub, just a tall barrel big enough to hold several cauldrons of hot water standing in the corner of the kitchen. After I had got in, the women still moved about in front of the barrel, while the woman from Liangjiashe kept adding water into the barrel with a gourd ladle. I was so embarrassed I ducked down each time she came close to me. Only after she had left the room with a bucket to feed the pigs did I quietly let out a sigh of relief. I had soaked for so long I was now dripping with sweat. The water must have been boiled with wormwood for the mosquito bites on my body had stopped itching. A lard lamp hung above me, emitting a pale blue glow in the steam, giving a blue tint to my body. Before I put on my shoes, I looked at this blue body of mine and was suddenly overcome with a peculiar feeling: the body seemed a stranger, seemed alien. I had no clothes on, and there was no one here but me, so no one to cover myself up for or pose for, not that I could have done so anyway. There was only my naked self, the reality of my own self. I had hands and legs, so I could do something; I had intestines and a stomach, so I had to eat something; and I had genitals, so I could produce children. For a while the world was shut outside the door; when I was out there I was always busy wherever

I went, and never had time to look at myself and think. The chance union of a sperm and an ovum had, in the distant past, brought one of my ancestors into existence; the chance meeting of this ancestor and another ancestor had brought about yet another fertilized ovum, making it possible for me to come into existence generations later. I, too, was a bluish fertilized ovum connected to a string of coincidences. What was I in this world for? What could I do? .... I was thinking too much, and too foolishly.

I started to wipe dry an inch-long scar on my calf. I had received the injury in a football pitch, where I was hit by a studded boot. But, no, I was wrong, it seemed. It seemed that I'd got the scar from a nasty bite by a short, dwarfish man. Was it on that rainy misty morning? On that narrow mountain track? He was coming towards me holding an opened umbrella and I was scowling at him. He was so frightened he started to shake. Then he went down on his knees and swore that he would never do it again, never, and that Second Sister-in-law's death had nothing to do with him, nor was he the one who had stolen Third Grandpa's buffalo. In the end he fought back, his eyes starting out of their sockets, and bit my leg. He jerked and pulled at the curb-rope round his neck. Then, abruptly, he stretched out his hands, and they began scratching and digging into the earth like two scuttling crabs. I didn't know how long it was before the scuttling crabs gave up their struggle and became quite still ....

I did not dare to think anymore. I didn't even have the guts to look at my hands .... Did they smell of blood and carry the marks of a cow rope cut deeply into the flesh?

No, I told myself with desperate finality, I'd never been here before, I'd never known any short, dwarfish man in my life. And I'd never seen any pale blue glow, not even in my dreams. Never.

The central room was now filling up with people. An old man came in, trampled out the pine torch, and said he had come to repay the two *yuan* he owed me for the cloth dye he had asked me to buy. He also invited me to dine and to "bed the night" in his place tomorrow. This led to a heated argument with Ai Ba who said that since he was going to fetch the tailor tomorrow and had already prepared the meat, I should go to his place tomorrow, there could be no question about it.

While they were still arguing, I slipped out of the house. Stumbling on the uneven road, I made my way towards the house "I" used to live in. I wanted to see it. Ai Ba said it was the cowshed behind the old tree. It had been converted into a cowshed only the year before last.

I walked past the tung trees again and once again I saw the weeds that were about to swallow up Old Grandpa — that silhouette of the tumbledown thatched hut. It was watching me quietly, coughing through the caw of the crows, whispering softly to me through the rustling leaves. I even felt a hint of alcoholic breath in the air.

You're back, my child? Grab yourself a chair and sit down. Didn't I tell you to go away, far, far away, and never come back again?

But I miss your pickled cucumber. I've tried to make some myself, but it isn't the same.

Why miss those humble things? I only made it because I knew you were starving and down on your luck. You worked in the fields all day, and you were so hungry you pulled the broad beans from the stalks and ate them raw.

You cared for us, I know.

Who doesn't have to be away from home sometime in his life? I know what it's like, I only did what I could.

I remember that day when we were sent to gather firewood. We only brought back nine loads, but you put it down as ten to give us more work points.

Is that so? I don't remember.

And you kept insisting we should shave off our hair. You said that hair and beards drank blood and that letting them grow was bad for our health.

Did I? I don't remember.

I should have come to see you earlier. It never occurred to me that things would have changed so much and that you'd be gone so soon.

It was time to go. If I'd lived on I'd have turned into a grand old monster. True, I loved a drink or two, but I've had enough and now I can sleep peacefully.

Won't you have a cigarette, Grandpa?

Go and put on the kettle if you want a cup of tea, Young Ma.

....

I left the smell of alcohol behind and moved on. Holding the guttering pine torch and thinking about what I had to do in the fields the next day, I made my way home, accompanied by the sound of frogs splashing into the pond. But now there was no pine torch in my hand and my home had turned into a cowshed. It looked so desolate, so unfamiliar. I could not see it clearly in the dark, I could only hear the cows chewing the cud and smell the strong odour of warm cow-dung on the straw in the shed. The cows took me for their master and the whole herd pressed forward, jostling one another, making the gate of the pen creak. As I walked, I heard echoes of my footsteps from the earthen wall of the shed, as if someone was walking on the other side of the wall, or perhaps even inside the clay of the wall. And that person knew my secret.

The dark mountain cliff opposite looked even more imposing and a lot closer at night, so close it suffocated you. It had curtained off the starry sky, leaving only a tiny uneven slit. Looking up at the tiny opening that was so high and so far away, I felt strongly the pull of the earth, as if I was being sucked in by a strange unknown force and was about to sink, sink into a deep crevice in the earth, down, down.

A huge moon appeared. The dogs in the village seemed frightened and started to whine. Treading on the moonlight seeping through the leaves, treading on tiny moonlit circles that were like algae, like duckweed, I went towards the stream. I thought to myself: there could be someone sitting by the stream, a young woman perhaps, with a leaf held between her lips.

There was no one by the stream. But on my way back, I saw the silhouette of someone under the old tree.

The night was so beautiful, it needed just such a silhouette to complete the picture.

"Is that you, brother Ma?"

"Yes." Surprisingly, I didn't feel at all flustered.

"Have you come from the stream?"

"You .... Who are you?"

"I'm Fourth Sister."

"Fourth Sister! How tall you've grown. I wouldn't have recognized you if I ran into you outside the village."

"You moved about in the big world, that's why you think everything has changed."

"How's your family?"

She suddenly went quiet and turned to look at the oil-press. When she spoke again, her voice was strained, "My sister, she hated you ...."

"Hated me ...." All tensed up, I darted a glance at the path leading to the light and the open space, ready to run. "It's ... it's hard to explain .... I've told her ...."

"Then why did you put corn into her basket that day? Didn't you know what that meant? How can you put things in a young woman's basket just like that? When she gave you a strand of her hair, didn't you know what that meant?"

"I ... I didn't understand. I didn't know your customs. I ... I wanted her to help me, so I let her carry a few cobs of corn."

Not a bad answer, I thought. I'd probably muddle through.

"Everyone was talking about the two of you. Were you deaf? I, too, saw you teaching her acupuncture. I saw it with my own eyes."

"She was keen. She wanted to be a doctor. Actually, I didn't know much about acupuncture then, I just messed about with the needles."

"You city people can't be trusted."

"Please don't say that!"

"It's true! It's true!"

"I know ..., your sister is a nice girl, I know. She sings beautifully and sews well. Once she took us to catch eels and she caught one every time she put her hand into the water. She cried when I was ill .... I know all that. But there are lots of things you don't understand, and it's hard to explain. I'll be busy rushing about all my life. I ... I've got my career."

So 'career' was the word I finally chose, although it sounded a bit awkward.

She covered her face and started to cry. "That man Hu, he was so vicious."

I thought I knew what she meant, so I ventured an answer, "So I've heard. I'll make him pay for it."

"But what's the use? What's the use?" She stamped her foot and cried even more disconsolately, "If you'd said a word or two in those days, things wouldn't have come to such an end. My sister has become a bird, she comes here day after day to call you, to call you. Can't you hear?"

I looked at her in the moonlight. Her thin gaunt back was heaving gently, the nape of her neck was smooth and the white scalp at the parting of her hair was shimmering in the dark. I really wanted to wipe away her tears, grab her by the shoulder, kiss the white scalp like I would my sister's, and let her salty tears drop onto my lips and swallow them.

But I checked myself; this was a strange story and I didn't dare to lick it lest it should burst.

There really was a lone bird calling in the tree. "Don't go, brother! Don't go, brother!" The sound, solitary, desolate, shot high into the sky like an arrow and then dropped swiftly into the mountains, into the forests, into the dark clouds in the distance and the noiseless thunder and lightning. I lit a cigarette, watching the storm.

"Don't go, brother! Don't go, brother!"

I left the village. Before I left, I wrote Fourth Sister a letter and asked the woman from Liangjiashe to pass it on to her. I said in the letter that her sister had wanted to be a doctor, and although she didn't become one in the end, I hoped Fourth Sister would fulfil her sister's wish. After all, one's life is in one's own hands. Would she like to sit the exam for the medical school? I'd send her lots of material to help her prepare for the exam, I promised. And I said I'd never forget her sister. I told her that Ai Ba had caught the parrot from the tree and I'd take it with me and let it sing everyday at my window and be my friend forever.

I felt as if I had run away from the village, for I left without saying goodbye to anyone, without taking the fragrant rice either. But what did I want the rice or the opium for? It seemed that I didn't come for those things. I felt suffocated — by the village, by my own inexplicable self. I had to run away. Turning back to take a last look at the village, I saw again the old tree that had been struck dead by lightning standing behind the blockhouse, its withered branches stretching out like convulsing fingers. The owner of those fingers had died in a battle and turned into a mountain, but he was still struggling to hold up his hands, to grasp at something.

I stopped at an inn in the county town and soon fell asleep amidst the babble of the parrot by my bedside. I had a dream. In it, I was on a dirt track in the mountain, walking. The track had been so badly washed out by water running down the slopes that it looked like a body stripped of skin and flesh, leaving exposed sticks of dry bones and lumps of shrivelled innards to bear the trampling of the straw sandals of the mountain folk. The road seemed to go on forever. I looked at my calendar watch — I had been walking for an hour, a day, a week ... but I was still on the same track. And no matter where I went afterwards, I always had this dream.

I woke with a start, got up three times to drink some water and went to the toilet twice. Finally, I phoned a friend. I had wanted to ask him whether he had managed to "wipe out" Mad Cao at cards, but I found myself talking to him about exams for self-study courses instead.

My friend called me "Huang Zhixian".

"What?"

"What do you mean what?"

"What did you call me?"

"Aren't you Huang Zhixian?"

"Did you call me Huang Zhixian?"

"Didn't I call you Huang Zhixian?"

I was stunned, my mind a complete blank. Oh yes, I was in an inn. In the passageway, mosquitoes and moths were fluttering about the dim light bulb, and there was a row of make-shift beds. Just beneath the mouthpiece of the phone there was a fat head snoring. But was there someone called Huang Zhixian in this world? And was this Huang Zhixian me?

I'm tired, I'll never be able to get away from that gigantic I! Mama!

January 1985

The Blue Bottle-cap

I gave up the struggle, handed him the wine bottle, and asked him if he could remove the bottle-cap. He was busy tackling a hunk of pig's trotter, his mouth full, a tendon caught between his teeth. Before he could answer, the bottle was gone.

A hand from my right had snatched it away. "Let me." The young village chief glanced at him and then at me, a good-natured smile on his ruddy face.

But the bottle had been snatched away too quickly and too abruptly to be a matter of polite helpfulness. It was obvious that something was not quite right.

The two men opposite me also looked a bit suspect; they cast him a glance and then gave me a smile.

He went on chewing hard at the pig's trotter. At last he belched contentedly, removed from his mouth a set of false teeth that could pass for real, carefully picked them clean, and then, stooping, went out to wash his hands. Only then did the village chief tap me on the knee and say, "You mustn't let him remove bottle-caps. Come, have some soup. It's delicious."

"Why not?"

"It's best not to mention bottle-caps."

"But why?"

"Come on. Have some soup, have some soup. Don't just eat plain rice."

I was perplexed. It had nothing to do with that remark about my eating rice, of course; it had to do with the empty seat on my left. He was there just now, in a pair of knee-length boots seldom seen in these parts, introducing himself as he helped me to some beef. "My name is Chen Mengtao, I'm the watchman in the tea storehouse." He also chatted to me for a while about the differences between spring tea and summer tea and about Emperor Wu of the Han dynasty. And I noticed he had placed a slim volume entitled *Stories of the Western Han Dynasty* in the crown of his felt hat. What was the special connection between him and bottle-caps?

When he had finished washing his hands he came back, a solemn look on his face. He snapped in his dentures, broke into a wrinkly grin, and resumed chatting with me about Emperor Wu. I shifted my chair back a little to get a better look at him and was a little horrified by his neck — slack skin round a bundle of protruding tubes that rose and fell softly as he spoke. It made the flesh creep on your own neck and you just wanted to hide it under your collar. His eyes gleamed with a kind of familiarity and fastened on to you like cat's eyes, with rings of yellow and green, rings which suggested great depth, that called to mind dark endless tunnels with specks of light beckoning to you, tempting you to go in.

I too felt there was something wrong.

When the village chief took me back to town, I asked him, "That man Chen, why can't he remove bottle-caps? Is he ...."

"I don't know. By the way, I hear that a red-haired wildman has just arrived at the municipal zoo. Have you seen it?"

"No. Why did Chen come here?"

"I haven't been here long, I don't know. D'you think there

really is such a creature as a red-haired wildman in this world? I bet it's just an ape."

I had to resign myself to talking about apes with him.

One day, I met another friend who also knew Chen Mengtao. Thanks to him, the bottle-cap in my heart was removed. It was after dinner and I was sitting on the veranda of an inn in the small town. Looking beyond the railing, I saw in the distance the old Fubo Temple and its ancient moss-mottled brick wall. Outside the high temple wall was an expanse of tiled eaves and sloping roofs, their ridges lying close together, some high, some low; some overlapping, some slightly apart. Wisps of cooking smoke were seeping out from the tile crevices and around the roof corners, curling into the sky, fading and then settling down on the open space along the streets, turning it into a sea of mist. And the roofs were like the masts of vessels sailing on the sea, while the raised ends of their ridges were like the bows and sterns of sailing ships.

I seemed to feel the floorboards swaying under my feet.

The young man who had just arrived worked at a meat and seafood supply centre. I had met him a few times before. He carried out research on people's surnames in his spare time and had come to the local police station to help with the census. I had been told that he could tell, just by glancing at the surname, whether the respondent had made a mistake about his place of origin and so had set straight many oversights and omissions in the records. He was held in high regard by various departments of the provincial government. For many years he had been working on a sort of unofficial history. He did it in secret and the records now filled half a trunk. He treasured these records and would probably want to bury them in one of the holy mountains. He had put down everything he thought worth recording, from the appearance of a mathematics whiz-kid in one village to the harvest of a king-size sweet potato in another and to rumours of agitation and growing unrest at some provincial institution of higher education. On hearing the name of Chen Mengtao, he puckered his lips in a smile, tossed his head backwards, rolled his eyes as if to look at me, or the ceiling, and spoke with the absolute certainty of someone who was in the know.

"Oh! Him. Well, I do know something about him. He came from a labour camp. Heard about the labour camps, haven't you? Used to be one here. A lot of these bricks and tiles came from there. They had a brick kiln there ...."

He went on (I've omitted some of his research details and explanations and am presenting his account with a touch of my own imagination where appropriate), — Chen Mengtao had, at one time, worked in a labour camp. His job was to carry rocks. He was tall, which put him at a disadvantage for the job. The carrying-pole worked like a lever. When the weight of the load was shifted onto his shoulder, the pole would come down on him like a mountain and bring him to his knees. In just a few days, he was bent double, he looked washed-out, his shoulders and back hurt, and he groaned with pain even when he stretched to change his clothes. And the clothes he took off were stiff and heavy, spotted and stained with rings of salt, each ring bigger than the other, residues of sweat fresh and stale. One morning, he woke up before daybreak because he wanted to go and empty his bladder, but his legs were so numb he couldn't move at all. He groped in the dark and found a pair of legs he presumed to be his. They were caked in mud for he had forgotten to wash them the night before. He tried but couldn't shift them. By the time he managed to struggle to the edge of the bed, he had peed, hot and steaming, into his pants, and wet the bed.

He broke down and sobbed, waking up the others in the shed, who cursed and swore at him.

He wanted to ask for an easier job. At that time, there was only one easy job — burying the dead. There were those who fell ill and died, and those who killed themselves. Then there were those who couldn't meet their work quotas and who were marched at gun point to training sessions. When patience ran out in these sessions, invariably things got a bit physical, and invariably, ropes and leather straps would be used. After a round of rather educative howling and screaming, there might well be some hundred pounds of flesh and bones to be returned to the earth. As Chen was always the first to arrive for assembly and instruction, and as he always bowed his head the lowest, the wardens often treated him kindly by sending him to bury the dead.

"Hey, you. Go and clean up," they would order him.

But Chen was terrified of the dead. In fact, just the howls of the other inmates would shake him like a leaf, contort his face with horror, and render him completely speechless. But then dead bodies are a lot lighter than rocks. Besides, dead bodies are supposed to bring bad luck and the wardens never bothered to watch the job done. So you could be at ease and take a nap in mid morning, you could even put on your socks and shoes, which you didn't normally do, and you could drink plenty of water, take plenty of rest, and be well away from the tension of the work site. You would be on the quiet and deserted hill slopes; you could take your time digging the hole in the ground, take your time filling up the grave. You could even sit on the handle of your rake until you had cooled off. And you could appreciate that without the weight of the carrying pole on your shoulder, without the blind menace of gun muzzles at your back, you could relax and grow plump.

With happy trepidation, Chen worked hard making ropes out of straw, putting to good use the straw used normally for tying millet and cushioning beds. At first, he had little idea how to roll the straw between his palms, but he was keen to learn and soon got the hang of it. When he finished making a rope, he would step on one end of it and pull hard to see if it could take the weight of a human body. Then he would test its strength on a carrying pole, after which he would hold up the rope to measure it against himself. Only when he was sure that it was two to three feet taller than himself would he be satisfied. As he worked, he would make a lot of noise to make the wardens notice him and to show that he could be trusted with the job.

But he had only to come before the icy body of the dead man and his wrinkled face would start to twitch. He held his breath, and it wasn't until he had turned his head away that he dared breathe again. Still, his hands would fail him and they couldn't even tie a knot properly. Fortunately, there was his mate. The man would tie two nooses, one to go round the neck of the dead body, another for the feet; and he would let Chen carry the fore end of the pole and go in front. There was no need to use a plank for although the human body is soft when it has a body temperature, it becomes hard and stiff when it is cold and can be lifted horizontally. Then, rocking and swaying, they carried the body up the hill and put it to eternal rest.

The good thing about walking in front was that you would be spared the sight of the dark hole that was the dead man's mouth, and the copper teeth inside, and the black shreds of pickled cabbage stuck between his teeth. You could tell yourself you were just carrying rocks, or even a bridal sedan chair. But the thought that behind your arse there moved, not a bridal sedan chair really but a bloke whose body, once warm and soft, had gone stiff and cold — the thought made Chen look dazed. One day when they were picking their way gingerly down a slope, Chen tried to skirt round a pile of cow-dung and slipped. The carrying pole was jolted violently and the dead man's hand fell from his chest and swung forward like a hammer, hitting the back of Chen's knee. It felt like someone was tickling him mischievously.

"My God!" Chen leapt up in the air, slipped and fell. The dead body also fell sideways and, as luck would have it, landed askew on Chen's stomach. He flung out his arms and fainted.

Chen's mate pressed the spot between his nose and his upper

lip and boxed his ears to bring him round. He came round eventually and spat out the sand on his lips.

After having done the job a few times, Chen gained in courage and became more experienced. He grew smarter, too. There simply was no need to dig the way he did the first time; the hole didn't have to be so big — he wasn't digging a swimming pool after all. There was no need to be particular either, no need to square the corners at the bottom of the pit. And when he went up and down the slopes, he knew precisely which foot to put on which slab of rock, and which to land on which clump of grass; he knew, too, which hand was to hold on to which bunch of weed or which tree branch. He also had more time to sit on the hillside resting on the handle of his rake. Chen had once acted in an amateur opera troupe. He remarked on his mate's fine and delicate features and said he could play the young male lead. He also told his mate that he had been in love with a woman whose name contained the character "tao", and that it was to show his fidelity that he called himself "Mengtao" (dreaming of "tao"). Oh yes, that was the truth. They chattered away about this and that until the wind turned chill, and the sun, a small white spot at first and then a huge flaming ball, sank behind the western hills. Then, casting a not uncompassionate glance at the work site in the distance, they packed up and made their way back. On meeting the others, they would quicken their pace and make like they had done a hard day's work. Back at the shed, it would be prudent not to talk too much, but to put the rakes, the carrying pole and the bundle of straw for making ropes back in the same position in the corner, to set them apart from the others' tools, and to have them ready for use the next time.

Every so often, they could even come back a little earlier than the others and slip to the kitchen to take a dish of pork and bean paste from the steamer. Then they would shut themselves up in the shed and gobble it up. They had obtained permission from the warden to do this, on the pretext that the job was bad for their health as they had to inhale the smell of the dead man and would therefore need a little more sustenance to keep them going. After all, they paid for the food with money sent from home.

In the same shed were a few inmates who were always behind with their work quota. Naturally, the bundle of straw in the corner filled them with trepidation. When they saw that Chen no longer wet his bed and was gaining more colour in his cheeks, they began to cast furtive glances at him, envy, mistrust and fear written all over their faces. For reasons Chen couldn't make out, his enamel bowl got badly chipped, and one of his old padded jackets vanished without a trace. If he was a little late for dinner, there would be nothing left in the pickle bowl, not even a trickle of sauce.

One day, a pair of chopsticks was left unused in the shed and a bed became empty. Everyone felt a little sad and stayed away from the emptiness and quietness of that bed. When his mate asked him to go and make some ropes, Chen didn't get up from the urine bucket; his cat eyes had lost their lustre, and his buck teeth were chattering, biting his lower lip.

"I ... I can't shit."

"Let's go and make some ropes."

"I can't ... I can't shit. What ... what am I going to do?"

His mate shot him a glance and saw why. Chen was a bag of nerves today probably because the man they had to put away was not like those they'd buried the last few times; he wasn't a stranger they'd never got to know but someone from the bed opposite Chen.

If the truth be told, Chen didn't know the man that well. He hadn't talked to him much. He had only borrowed a pair of trousers from him the morning he wet his bed and chatted once to him about dumplings sold at an old restaurant in town. They got on fairly well but were far from being friends. Still, they had slept in beds across from each other for a few months, and just the night before last, Chen had cursed when he was woken up by the sound of the man grinding his teeth. Today the bed was empty. And now

Chen had to make a rope for the head that used to grind its teeth .... Did he really have to? The bloke wouldn't be grinding his teeth on his arse, would he?

Chen's mate said, "I see you don't want to go. OK. Go talk to the chief and get someone to replace you."

Chen clenched his teeth and said, staring at a worn-out straw sandal in front of the make-shift bed, "I'll go and carry rocks. I ... I'll carry rocks!"

"Carry rocks! You skinny monkey? I'll probably have to come and carry you tomorrow!"

"I ... I'm stronger than Song."

"They've increased the work quota today!"

"By how much?"

"Thirty cubic feet per person."

"My God!"

Chen changed colour, his face an agonized grimace, and he felt even more desperate and bunged up. He straightened his back, craned his neck, wrinkled his nose and shut his eyes, but there was no relief. He knew that the others had started work quite a while ago, even if he had three heads and six arms, he couldn't complete the quota. And the urine bucket ....

"D'you think," Chen gasped, "D'you think we have to bury him today?"

"What else can we do? Consecrate him?"

"Are we going to cover him ... with soil?"

"What else? With rice?"

"In ... in the same place?"

"What the hell are you on about? Forget it if you don't want to come. But don't waste my time, I've got to make some ropes."

"To tell you the truth, I really ..., really, my legs are like jelly. Just think, the day before yesterday I heard him grinding his teeth, yesterday, he smiled at me .... Look, that's his pair of chopsticks on the shelf above my bed. They're staring hard at me! I can't carry him, I really can't. Don't be mad at me, I can't ..."

He did go, but he ate nothing when he came back to the shed.

Life gradually returned to normal, as if nothing extraordinary had ever taken place. As usual, they ate squatting on their heels, shovelling rice into their mouths; as usual, they groaned with stiff limbs; as usual, they scratched themselves, killed and flicked away a bedbug or two. As for the pair of unused chopsticks, someone had turned them into anchor nails for his carrying pole. Every day the sun's rays reached in through the door like a huge white tongue and licked away some of the damp, the smell of straw, taking them back to nature, melting them into the fragrance of vegetable flowers and the occasional cries of wild geese.

Chen was becoming a little peculiar; he seemed distracted, and would often cast a suspicious glance at his mates. At dinner, he would look up for no reason, bare his buck teeth, and study the faces before him one by one. Even though he never examined you for long, you still felt that he had looked deep into you and was sizing you up for some undisclosed purpose. He gave you the shivers.

He also became very keen on doing people favours and was especially attentive to those who had difficulty completing their work quota. On waking up at night, he would toss and turn, and then tiptoe to your bed, pick up your shoes and arrange them more neatly side by side; or he would top up your tea mug; or perhaps correct your sleeping posture by shifting your head or your feet ever so gently. If he woke you in a moment of carelessness, he would bow and nod his head and grin at you, baring his buck teeth — his unique way of saying hello, sorry and goodnight. The lines that appeared on his face when he grinned would disappear so sudden-ly, so quickly, so mechanically that you could not but sense some-thing malicious in them. His cat eyes, grown used to gazing at the ropes and the pit, looked even more deep set. The pupils seemed to have diffused into rings of yellow, behind which green specks glimmered. When his eyes met yours, you would feel he had seen through you and worked out everything — your weight and the thickness of your neck, even the way you would lie stretched out in future — and he had secretly measured your height against a certain something.

He drove people up the wall with his solicitous attention and abject timidity. Once, a burly fellow was woken up from his sleep by the sound of Chen's breathing. He shot up, backed away several feet and snarled, "Fuck off Chen, you goddamn son of a bitch. Why for God's sake do you fiddle with my shoes? Damn it, why mine?"

"Oh —, there was some straw in your shoes."

"What's that got to do with you? Fuck off."

Chen bowed, smiled wryly, turned round to pick up someone's soiled shirt and a cake of soap, and was about to go and wash it in the pond outside.

The owner of the shirt, too, was taken aback. In a trembling voice, he said, "Chen ... Chen Mengtao ..., I've never done you wrong. What're you doing with my shirt?"

"Oh —, I ... I was about to give it a wash."

"What d'you mean by that? What do you mean?"

Chen was upset and thought it must be that the service he provided wasn't good enough. He scrambled into bed in a huff, and tossed and turned, now and then letting out a sigh. Some people look huge when they are lying in bed. Strangely, Chen seemed to shrink when he was under the quilt; he looked like a child.

He suffered more and more from baffling, inexplicable bouts of guilt, and the more solicitous he tried to be, the more he was cursed. His hair had turned visibly grey; he looked pallid, the sockets of his eyes sunken in his gaunt face, and he went about flustered and jumpy. But he persisted. When he delivered lunch to the work site, he would, for no reason at all, break into a brisk walk before slowing down to his normal pace again, as if someone invisible had just trodden on his heels. When he was in the shed, he would always volunteer to take the urine bucket out for cleaning. Tall and clumsy in movement, he often spilled the stinking mess onto his shoes and his trousers, but he never complained. One blustery day, the temperature had dropped so low everyone felt numb at the fingertips and the nose, even getting in and out of bed was a real torment. The wardens had a word among themselves and agreed to let the inmates buy some wine to keep out the cold. Chen at once took out all the money his brother had sent him and scuttled to the storekeeper to get some wine.

He came back with the bottle and tried to remove the small metal bottle-cap. He used his teeth, it didn't work. He tried forcing it open with a chopstick, but it stayed firmly in place. Finally, he held a hoe between his knees and used its blade to pry off the cap. There was a loud click and the cap flew into the air and disappeared.

For a while he was lost in amazement. Then he muttered, "Where's the cap?"

"Where's the cap?" He looked under the straw mat, picked up each of his shoes and turned them over.

"Where's the cap?" With a clatter he pushed aside the rakes and the carrying poles at the corner of the wall, and glanced at the empty urine bucket. But he couldn't find it.

The others had had a few quick swigs at the bottle and were feeling on their cheeks the rush of warmth from their stomach. Realizing that Chen hadn't joined them yet, they turned round to look for him. They didn't see the upper part of his body, just his bottom sticking up in the air. As usual, the back seam in the middle of his trousers was pulled to one side, and there were two faint mud marks where his buttocks were. Then the two mud marks went straight out of the shed to the yard outside, onto the road beyond .... Later, it was said that he had even tried to get past the sentry post and head for the town. And he kept mumbling to himself in disbelief:

"Where's the cap? It's really weird. Where's my bottle-cap?"

Chen had gone mad, just like that. Calmly and amiably, he began to look for the bottle-cap that would never be found. He left everyone puzzled and bewildered.

Time passed, many died and many were born, houses were demolished and houses were built. Later, much later, when the labour camps were finally abolished, Chen was set free and his sentence overturned, along with many other cases like his. He was sent to one hospital after another. Eventually, he seemed to have sufficiently recovered to be assigned to his present post at the tea storehouse. He received a decent salary, ate steamed pork with bean paste, read newspapers or a book or two occasionally, listened to the radio, commented on the performance of amateur operatic troupes, and once in a while went to a store in his knee-high boots to buy a copy of a popular science magazine. Apart from his fixation with bottle-caps, he seemed quite normal. Many people had, out of kindness or maliciousness, shown him all sorts of bottle caps. He held each up with his coarse fingers, studied it with meticulous care, and turning his richly-coloured cat eyes to the bottle-cap bearer, he would deliver his opinion as seriously as if he was discoursing on an academic topic, "This looks rather like it. But this is not it."

Nobody knew which one he was looking for.

— The amateur expert on surnames had finished his story. He looked at his watch and said, "Well, I've talked too much. I'd like to hear the latest from you. Anything interesting?"

I lit a cigarette. It dawned on me that after all, we were just having a chat. And since we were just chatting, the substance of our conversation carried little or no significance. We could change the topic and chat about something else, about surnames, about pig's trotters, about nuclear disarmament. It was just a chat after all.

My mind suddenly went blank; for a long time I couldn't think of a single topic, or a single sentence, or even a single word.

I saw again the roofs floating on the clouds of smoke rising from the kitchens. Below the roofs lived the people and their families, hundreds and thousands of them. Over the years, these roofs had sailed here from I know not where and dropped anchor, forming a market town. Maybe some day in future they would set sail again in different directions and put into port somewhere else to set up new worlds. Quietly they had come, quietly they would go. For the moment they were taking a rest in this small haven, they had pulled up their oars and were basking in the soothing blue peace and quiet of the place. Would they set sail again the next morning? — I studied them carefully. No, not a single word.

As if the bottle-cap had gone missing.

January 1985

Pa Pa Pa

1

When he was born, he showed no sign of life for two whole days, his eyes remained closed, and he refused to feed, scaring his folks out of their wits. It was not until the third day that he started to cry. Later on when he could crawl, the villagers often played with him, teaching him this and that. Very soon, he picked up two expressions, one was "Papa", the other was "F___ Mama". The second was a vulgar expression but coming from a toddler, it didn't really mean anything and could simply be taken as a sign, a symbol, what you will. You could, for example, take it to mean "F___ haha". Time passed; he was three, then five, then seven or eight years old; but still these were the only words he could say. Besides, his eyes were dull, his movements slow; and his head was big, fleshy, and lopsided, like a green gourd turned upside-down. Anyway, it passed for a head, whatever oddities there were inside it. After each meal, he left the house, a grain or two of rice sticking to the corners of his mouth, a large oily stain on his chest, and rocking and swaying, tottered up and down the village, greeting passers-by of all ages and sexes with a cordial "Papa". If you scowled at him, he would return the compliment at once — staring at a certain point on your head, he would slowly roll his eyes skyward, showing the whites of his eyes, and then spit out the words, "F___ Mama." Then he would turn and make his escape. It was no easy job for him to roll his eyes: it seemed as if he had to mobilize all the muscles of his neck, chest and abdomen before he could manage it. Turning his head was an equally laborious job. His neck was weak, and his head had to roll like a pepper grinder, tracing a big arc before steadying into the turn. But running took the most effort. He stumbled and staggered, and had to thrust the weight of his head and chest forward to drag the rest of him along. To get his direction, he had to strain to see from under his brows. Every stride was huge — he was like a sprinter approaching the finishing line in slow motion.

He had to be given a name — for use at formal celebrations and for his tombstone. And so he came to be called "Young Bing".

Young Bing had a lot of "papas", but he had never seen his real father. The story had it that his father, tired of his ugly-looking wife and fed up with the monstrosity she had given birth to, had long left the village to become an opium trader and had never been back. Some said he had been killed by bandits, others would have it that he was running a bean curd shop in Yuezhou,[1] yet others would tell you that he led a wild life, had squandered all his money on women, and had been seen begging on the streets of Chenzhou. Anyway no one could say for sure whether he actually existed; it had become a mystery of little importance.

Young Bing's mother grew vegetables and raised chickens for a living, in addition to being a midwife. Women often came to her

---

[1] In its archaic sense, "Zhou" refers to an administrative division in ancient China. The writer's repeated use of this word in its archaic sense is part of his overall strategy to show that the characters lead a life that seems to have remained untouched by the passage of time and the process of modernization in China.

house and talked to her in hushed voices. After a while, she would pick up her scissors and all and go out with her visitor, the two still whispering into each other's ears. That pair of scissors had been used for cutting shoe patterns and pickles, and for trimming nails; it had also delivered a whole new generation to the mountain villages, ensuring the future of the place. She had cut the umbilical cords of many a young life at birth but the lump of flesh she herself had brought into the world would never make a man. She had visited all sorts of herbal medicine specialists, made offerings to the gods, and prostrated herself before deities of wood and clay. Still, she didn't manage to teach her son another phrase to say. Rumour had it that years ago, she had killed a spider while chopping some firewood in the kitchen. The spider had green eyes, a red body the size of a clay pot, and its web was the length of a bolt of cloth. When it was thrown into the fire, a nauseous stench enveloped the village for three days. It was obvious she'd offended a spider demon and Sig ? was being punished through her son. Nothing unusual about that.

It wasn't clear whether the story reached her ears. Anyway she also had a break-down once and was forced to swallow a mouthful of faeces. She recovered and even began to gain weight. Now, she was the size of the roller on the threshing floor, tyres of fat drooping from her waist. Like her son, she, too, occasionally rolled her eyes.

Mother and son lived in a solitary timber hut on the edge of the stockaded village. Like all the other houses, the beams and pillars were thicker and heavier than necessary, for the trees in the region were not worth a penny. Bedclothes and colourful children's clothes, with urine stains shaped like lotus leaves, were often hung outside the house to dry. The stains were of course the legacy of Young Bing. He often amused himself in the yard in front of the house, poking earthworms or rolling chicken droppings in his palms. When he got bored, he would take his runny-nosed self off to see if he could catch sight of anybody. On spying a few lads returning from felling trees up the mountain or setting out to

"chase meat", he would smile at their ruddy faces and greet them
with a friendly "Papa —."

A burst of laughter. And the ruddy-faced lad on whom Young
Bing's eyes were fixed would go up to him, huffing and puffing, and
call him names or shake his fist at him. Or he would give Young
Bing a sharp rap on his gourd-like head with his knuckles.

Sometimes, the lads would poke fun at one another. Laughing,
one would seize Young Bing by the arm and point a finger at his
mate, coaxing him, "Say Papa. Come on, say Papa." If Young Bing
hesitated, the lad would sometimes press a few slices of sweet potato
or a handful of baked chestnuts into his hands. After Young Bing
had obliged them they would, as usual, laugh heartily and Young
Bing would, as usual, be rapped on the head or have his ears boxed.
If he paid them back with an angry "F___ Mama", the world would
spin before his eyes, and his face and head, already smarting, would
burn.

The two expressions seemed to have different meanings, but as
far as Young Bing was concerned, they produced the same effect.

He knew how to cry. He burst into tears.

Mother came. Shaking her fist at the lads, she pulled Young
Bing away. Sometimes, she would let loose a torrent of abuse at the
lads, slapping her hands, slapping her thighs, her hair in a mess.
After each volley of abuse, she would wipe her hands on the inside
of her thighs — a gesture which was supposed to add strength to
the vicious power of the words. "Blast you! A plague upon you. May
your blasted heads be chopped off. You heartless louts. This one
here is thick in the head. And you bully him. It's wicked, wicked!
Watch, you gods in heaven, open your eyes! Could these scoundrels
have wriggled their way out of their mama's womb without my help?
They eat rice like everyone else, but they're rotten through and
through. Rotten and infected with evil! They aren't even grown
men, but watch how they bully my child!"

She was not a native of the place; she had married into the

village. Her strange accent amused the lads. They didn't mind her
as long as she didn't curse them with the expression, "birds behind
time", which was supposed to mean "without heirs". They would just
laugh and then scurry off.

Shouting, crying; crying and shouting — so the days went on,
there was enough excitement to make life worth living even as one
grumbled about it. One after another, the lads found bristles
growing on their chins; slowly, their backs began to arch. Another
batch of snot-nosed kids grew into lads. Young Bing, however, was
still no taller than a pack-basket, and he still wore a child's red-floral
open-crotch pants. For many years, his mother had been telling
people he was "only thirteen", but he had aged visibly and faint lines
began to mark his forehead.

At night, she often closed the door, made Young Bing sit at her
feet by the fire, and then murmured to him. The things she said,
her tone of voice, even the way she sat rocking gently in the bamboo
chair, were typical of a mother talking to a child. "You're a naughty
boy. What use will you be? You don't listen to your mama, you don't
do what mama tells you. You eat plenty but you never learn a thing.
Better to raise a dog than to raise you, a dog can guard the house.
Better to raise a pig than to raise you, a pig can give me meat. Oh
dear! Oh dear! You naughty boy, what good are you? Not even a
grain's worth of good. And what's the use of that dicky of yours?
What woman would marry you ... H'm?"

Staring at this motherly mama, at her gleaming dead-fish eyes,
Young Bing wet his lips with his tongue and, finding the droning
all too familiar, spat out the words excitedly, "F___ Mama."

But mother had heard the expression too often to feel offended. She went on rocking to and fro, and the bamboo chair creaked
softly.

"Will you still care about Mama when you've found yourself a
wife?"

"F___ Mama."

"Will you still care about Mama when you have kids?"

"F___ Mama."

"Will you look down on your Mama and treat her like dog shit when you become a high official?"

"F___ Mama."

"You have a sharp tongue, don't you? It does nothing but swear at people."

Young Bing's mother laughed, her eyes narrowing into slits, her neck thickening under her double-chin. To her, such behind-closed-doors dream-talk was a privilege no one could take away from her.

2

The village perched high in the mountains above the clouds. When you left the house, you often found yourself stepping into rolling clouds. Take a step forward, and the clouds would retreat, while those at your back would move in behind you, bearing you up on a solitary island without end, floating. You never felt lonely on the island. Sometimes you caught sight of the armoured birds on the trees. Black as coal and the size of a thumb, their call was loud and clear and rang with a metallic twang. They seemed to have remained unchanged since time immemorial. Sometimes you would see a gigantic shadow drifting towards you on the clouds, a shadow like two open pages of a book. At first glance, it looked like an eagle; on closer examination, you realized it was a butterfly. At first glance, it was greyish black; on closer examination, you found that the black wings had green, yellow and orange markings, as well as spots and lines so faint they looked like indecipherable hiero-glyphics. Most people, however, paid no attention to these things, nor were they interested; they just hurried on. If they felt they had lost their way, they would pee on the ground and start cursing and swearing, which was said to be the best way of shaking off the demons that had led them astray.

Splashing and dripping, the steaming urine rained into the clouds. What happened below the clouds was of no consequence to the inhabitants of the mountain villages. In the Qin dynasty, the government had set up a county in this region. In the Han dynasty, the government had also set up a county here. Later on, during the Ming dynasty and the Qing dynasty, administrative and other major reforms had been introduced .... But all these accounts came from the lips of cattle-hide dealers and opium traders plying their trade in the mountains. And for all that had been said about government policies and reforms, the people still had to depend on themselves for their livelihood.

Growing crops was reality for the people; so were snakes and insects and miasma and malaria. The mountains abounded with snakes, some as big around as a bucket, some as thin as bamboo chopsticks. They often slithered through the bushes by the road-side, and a passing cattle-hide dealer who thought he had sighted a prey would be dealt a nasty blow. It was said that snakes were lascivious creatures and that if you locked a snake up in a cage and placed it in front of a woman, it would writhe and arch up and down in the cage until it exhausted itself. Extracting the gall bladder of a snake is no easy job. If you knock a snake on the head, its gall bladder will drop to its tail; if you attack its tail, the gall bladder will shoot up to its head. If you take too long about it, the gall bladder will burst and become useless. The usual trick is to tie a bundle of straw into the shape of a woman and splash it with paint. If the trick worked and the snake twined itself round the straw figure, you could then slash open the snake's abdomen and extract its gall bladder. The snake, in its excitement, wouldn't even notice it. Then there was the poisonous worm. Its victim's eyeballs would turn greenish yellow, his fingers black. The taste of raw beans wouldn't seem bitter to him; even the bitter rhizome of Chinese goldthread wouldn't

make him wince. If he ate fish, there would be a live fish in his belly;
if he ate chicken, he would have a live chicken inside him. The cure
was to kill a white cow and drink the fresh blood, but you had to
crow like a cock three times before you drank it. As for the dense
trees on the mountains, they were what the villagers depended on
for their lives when the mountain passes were blocked by heavy
snow. At times like this, no one could survive if he didn't keep a fire
going in his house. There was no need to cut firewood. Logs were
thrust whole through the door into the fire and left to burn section
by section until they were spent. Then there was a type of tree with
tall straight trunks which grew skyward for tens or even hundred of
feet before shooting out into branches. In ancient times, tax-collec-
tors often made special trips to the mountains to exact corvee from
the peasant by ordering them to fell these trees and deliver the
timber to the counties for use in the officials' residences as beams
and columns — an imposing reminder of the power and prestige
of the feudal bureaucrats who lived there. Nowadays, the mountain
folk would cut the wood into planks for boats which they would
deliver all the way to Chenzhou or Yuezhou. The "people down
there" would saw up the timber, which they called "scented *nan*",
and use it to make lattice windows or make-up boxes. But the
journey down the mountain was full of hazards. If you ran into
another group of peasants offering sacrifice to the rice god, they
might well chop off your head and offer that as well. If you ran into
bandits, you would lose not only your purse but also your boat. Then
there were women who caught poisonous insects of all sorts using
cock's blood for bait. They ground the dried insects into powder
and hid it in their fingernails. When your attention was elsewhere,
they would flick the powder into your teacup, causing you to die a
sudden death. This was called "casting the insect spell". It was
believed that those who did this would gain longevity and good
health. Most young men, therefore, would not venture far from
their villages unless they had to, and even if they did, they wouldn't

dare to drink just any water. They would make sure there were live fish in a pond before they helped themselves to a few mouthfuls. Once, two men who were not dressed warmly enough took shelter from the cold in a cave. Groping their way in, they reached the end of the cave and found a pile of human bones. On the walls patterns had been carved with knives. They looked like birds, like animals, like a map, like squiggles, but they were indecipherable. Who could know what had happened there?

The steep ridges and deep gorges also made it difficult to transport heavy timber, and so most of the trees were left untouched. They grew in majestic splendour, competing for sunlight and rain and mist, and then died quietly in the mountains. The branches fell and rotted on the ground, the layers thickening year by year. When trod upon, they oozed black slime and a few air bubbles, exuding a pungent smell of damp and rot that hung so heavy in the air it enveloped the wailings of generations of wild boars.

It enveloped the villages too, and blackened them.

There was no knowing where these villagers had come from. Some said Shaanxi, others said Guangdong — all conjectures only. They spoke a language quite different from that spoken by the peasants of Qianjiaping at the foot of the mountain. For example, they still used a lot of archaic words — they said "watch" instead of "see" or "look", "speak" instead of "say", "lean" instead of "stand", "lie down" instead of "sleep". And they used the word "*qu*" as a pronoun to refer to someone nearby. They also had an unusual way of addressing their relatives. The emphasis seemed to be on unity — the unity of a large family — for there was a deliberate confusion of the distinctions between close and distant relatives: they addressed their father as "uncle", their uncle as "father", their elder sister as "elder brother", their sister-in-law as "elder sister", and so on. The term "papa" came by way of Qianjiaping and was not widely used. According to the prevailing custom, therefore, the man who had left Young Bing and his home and was heard of no more ought to be Young Bing's "uncle".

But this had little to do with him.

A more detailed and authoritative account of the history of their ancestors was preserved in the ancient songs that still survived. Dusk came early in these parts and during the long evenings, the villagers would stroll over to their neighbour's and sing a song or two, tell stories, chat about farm work, tell tales about the bandits, doze, or do nothing. The most popular places to while away an evening were, of course, the houses of well-off families, where the sideboards and stoves were beautifully polished with lard. The walls were sometimes fitted with an oil lamp whose flames, fed by wild boars' grease, cast a faint ghastly blue haze over everything. And sometimes reddish-brown light beams spilled from a wire lamp-basket inside which pine rosin burned. The burning rosin would pop, and in the flickering light, the wire basket would look as if it was twitching in its sleep. There was always a fire burning in the brazier, to keep out the cold in winter and to drive away the mosquitoes in summer. The fumes had turned the beams and the ceiling charcoal black, so that you couldn't tell the beams from the ceiling. There was a cold acrid smell of smoke everywhere. Pieces of grey string hung from the ceiling. When fanned by the heat rising from the fire, they let drop a sprinkle of ashes that danced and drifted in the air before settling unnoticed on people's heads and shoulders and knees.

Delong was the best singer. He had faint eyebrows and no beard, and led a wild life. At the mention of his name, the women would grin and start cursing him. His voice was small and high-pitched — a woman's voice. When he broke into his nasal tunes, it was like a knife inside your head turning and twisting and scraping, sending chills up and down your body. Everyone admired him. What a voice Delong had!

He would just drop in, playing with a poisonous green snake whose fangs had been knocked out, grin cheekily at the jibes thrown

at him, and without much persuasion, he would fix his gaze on the
beams, pinch his throat once or twice, and start to sing in earnest:

> Are there many houses in Chenzhou?
>
> Many pillars and many beams?
>
> Are there many birds in Mt. Cock?
>
> Many nests and many feathers?

Apart from these impromptu "nonsense ditties", the songs that
amused the folks most were his raunchy love songs. He enjoyed
singing them too (I shall refrain from citing the really bold ones):

> I miss you, I miss you, I miss you my man,
>
> Walking or sleeping I miss you bad,
>
> Walking I leave you room by my side,
>
> In bed I leave you room to abide.

When there was a celebration or a sad event, or on New Year's
Day and other festivals, everyone in the village would observe an
age-old custom and sing "*Jian*", meaning sing about ancient times
and the dead. They first sang about their fathers, then about their
grandfathers, then about their great-grandfathers, and so on, going
all the way back to Jiangliang. Jiangliang was our forefather, but he
came after Fufang, who came after Huoniu, who came after Younai.
Younai was descended from his parents. And who gave birth to
Younai's father? It was Xingtian — maybe he was the Xingtian
mentioned in Tao Qian's poem, who "fights fiercely for his lofty
aspirations". When Xingtian was born, the sky was like a vast
expanse of white mud, the earth a vast expanse of black mud, the
two glued so tightly together even a mouse couldn't squeeze
through. Xingtian raised his axe in one mighty blow and severed
heaven from earth. But he packed too much force into his blow,
and his axe swung round and lopped off his head as well. From then
on he used his nipples for eyes and his navel for a mouth. He
laughed till the earth shook and the mountains swayed; he swung
his axe and with mighty blows, knocked the sky upwards for three
years until it reached its present height. He hammered down the

earth for another three years until it descended to its present level.

And how did Xingtian's descendants come to settle here? — It was a long long time ago. The fifth matriarch and the sixth patriarch as well as their descendants were living together on the shores of the East Sea. As the family swelled and the clan grew bigger and bigger, the place became so crowded there wasn't even an open space the size of a mat. Five of the women who married into the clan had to share one pestle room for grinding grain, and there was only one water bucket to be shared among six unmarried daughters. How could life go on like that? And so, at the suggestion of Phoenix, they picked up their hoes and rakes and set off in the direction of West Mountain, travelling in maple-wood boats and *nan*-wood boats. With Phoenix leading the way, they found the glittering River of Gold. But gold mines, however precious, can be exhausted; so they moved on and found the dazzling River of Silver. But silver mines, however valuable, can also be exhausted; so they moved on again until finally they found the glorious River of Rice. Oh! Rice, River of Rice! They could bring up their children on rice. And so everyone went there, laughing, rejoicing, singing:

> Grandma led the clan, Oh, from the east afar,
> Grandpa left the east, Oh, a long long line behind,
> On and on they went, Oh, the mountains were so
>   high,
> They turned back to look, Oh, their homes behind
>   the clouds.
> On and on they went, Oh, through a gap in the sky,
> Grandma and grandpa, Oh, their hearts were heavy,
> To the west of them, Oh, the mountains stretched so
>   far,
> The road grew weary, Oh, was the end not near?
>   ....

It was said that an official historian had once visited Qianjiaping and pronounced that there was no truth to the peasants' songs. The official said that Xingtian's head was chopped off by Huangdi when the two were fighting for the throne. The four big families of the region — the Peng, Li, Ma, and Mo clans — had come from the area of Yunmengze and not from "the shores of the East Sea". It was when war broke out between the early kings, Huangdi and Yandi, that the refugees fled southwest along the five rivers into the land of the barbarians. The strange thing is, there is not the slightest reference to the terrors of war in the ancient songs.

But the folks of Cock's Head Village never cared for the words of the official historian. Instead, they believed what Delong's ancient songs told them, even though they were none too fond of Delong's faint eyebrows. Eyebrows faint as water presaged a poor, lonely life.

Having entertained his folks with his songs for over a decade, Delong left with his small green snake.

He was probably Young Bing's father.

3

Young Bing loved looking at people and was particularly interested in strangers. If he ran into an artisan entering the village, he would go up and call him, "Papa." If the artisan didn't mind him, Young Bing's mother would, half bashfully and half beaming with pride, shout at Young Bing in a tone at once forgiving and reproachful, "Don't be daft!"

Then, she, too, would laugh.

The kiln master had come to the village. Young Bing wanted to go to the kiln with him; but the kiln master wouldn't hear of it because of a rule laid down in ancient times. Legend had it that the wise and resourceful Zhuge Liang, a great statesman and strategist in the Three Kingdom's period (220-265), had passed through this region as he led his troops southwards, and had taught the peasants how to build kilns. Since then, the kiln masters would, whenever they visited this place, hang up a picture with the *taiji* sign[2] and then prostrate themselves in worship before starting the kilns. Lighting the fire was an art, for there was a difference between a *yin* fire and a *yang* fire. When the fire was lit, the kiln master would fan it gently with a goose-feather fan — Didn't the wise Zhuge Liang always carry a goose-feather fan?

Women and children were forbidden to go near the kilns while the lads sent to carry bricks were forbidden to use foul language. These rules gave the kiln master an aura of mystery. At break time, the lads would gather round him, offer him cigarettes, and enquire respectfully about the outside world. Shiren was probably the most courteous of them all towards the kiln master. With lavish hospitality, he would invite the kiln master home for a "meat meal" and to "bed the night". But of course that was because he was by no means master of the house, and so he simply didn't have to keep his word.

Shiren was nicknamed "Idiot Ren", he was getting on in years but was still a bachelor. He often stole into the wood and hid himself near the stream where the young women went to bathe, their laughing, screaming white shadows delighting and tormenting him. But his eyes were poor and he couldn't see clearly. To ease his frustration, he often watched the little girls peeing by the roadside, or peered at a certain part of a bitch or a cow. Once, he was studying a cow with a stick when Young Bing's mother walked past. The woman loved to stir things up; as soon as she was back at the village, she let loose her long tongue and started whispering into people's ears, her eyebrows dancing. Only when she saw Idiot Ren in the

---

[2]An ancient Chinese diagram which explains the phenomena of the universe. It comprises two halves — the ultimate principles of *yin* and *yang* — locked in unison in a circle. Outside the circle are drawn hexagrams in eight directions: the cardinal points and the half-cardinal points. The *taiji* sign is a symbol used in the Taoist religion. Zhuge Liang was a famous military strategist of the Three Kingdoms period.

distance did she collect herself and walk away, calm and composed. Since then, Idiot Ren found that no matter where he went — digging bamboo shoots or collecting pine rosin up the mountains, or attending to the fodder in the cow shed, the woman was just round the corner, pretending to be looking for some medicinal herbs or what not, her dead-fish eyes glancing smugly in his direction. Idiot Ren was furious, and yet he could find no pretext to explode. He swore and cursed at no one in particular, but it brought him no relief. So he took it out on Young Bing. If he ran into Young Bing when his mother was not around, and if no one else was around, he would box Young Bing's ears ruthlessly.

The little old man was used to such treatment; he could take it. His mouth twitched, but no pain showed on his face.

Idiot Ren didn't stop until his fingers started to hurt.

"F___ Mama, f___ Mama ...." When the little old man realized that things didn't bode well for him, he took to his heels.

Idiot Ren overtook Young Bing and, seizing him by the nape of his neck, forced him to kneel down and kowtow to him till grains of sand got stuck in his forehead.

Young Bing burst into tears. But tears were useless — Idiot Ren knew all too well that by the time Young Bing's mother arrived, he'd be gone and the half mute couldn't tell on him. And so Idiot Ren took his revenge time and again. What the mother owed him, he took it back with full interest from the son, and he never had to suffer any consequences.

Young Bing's mother came back from the vegetable garden and found Young Bing crying. Thinking that he had been bitten or had got himself badly scratched, she examined him for wounds. When she couldn't find any, she screamed at him, gnashing her teeth, "Go on, cry yourself to death! You can't walk without stumbling, but you're out all day like a wild brat. So you fell and hurt yourself! Serves you right!"

At times like this, Young Bing would fly into a rage. He would roll his eyes until the pupils disappeared, the veins on his forehead all stood out, and he would bite his hands and tear his hair as if he had gone mad.

Onlookers would sigh, "Better if he were dead!"

Later on, for some strange reason, Idiot Ren got very friendly with Young Bing's mother. He called her "aunt", his voice ever so sweet. And when he helped her husk rice with mortar and pestle or mend a bucket, he would always attack the job with gusto. When the villagers spread idle rumours about her, he would leap to her defence and try to get to the bottom of things. Needless to say, this stirred up no end of suspicion. Gossips never leave a widow in peace; so it was inevitable that Idiot Ren and his "aunt" should begin to hear stories and that the women should point their fingers at them.

Young Bing's mother looked at Idiot Ren with narrowed smiling eyes as she tried to work out ways of finding him a wife. As a midwife, she often went to other villages and knew a lot of women. She approached a few families, but none would send her the horoscope of a prospective bride. It didn't really surprise her though. In recent years, Cock's Head Village had fallen on hard times and there were many bachelors beside Idiot Ren. For a number of years, therefore, Idiot Ren held little hope of getting married and he aged gradually. He had heard that there was a kind of "flower spell" which could make a woman fall in love with you — you need only get a hair from the head of the woman you fancied, tie it to a leaf on a tree outside your house, and when the breeze blew, repeat the spell seventy-two times. He tried it, but it didn't work.

Idiot Ren had something of a squint and until he saw you clearly, he always looked as though he was angry. When he could see you, he would flash you a smile, and depending on what you said, he would look surprised, infuriated, sorry, or even dignified and compassionate. As he nodded his head, the black mole at the nape of his neck rose and fell. He was especially fond of rubbing shoulders with people above the common run, like kiln masters, saw masters, merchants, scholars, fortune tellers and so on. When he talked to them, he always spoke forrmal Mandarin. After a round of flattery, he would hint subtly to them that he was well-versed in history and knew about quite a few of the peasant heroes that had risen in rebellion in the Sui dynasty (581-618). At times, he would even fish out from his pocket a piece of paper with the first line of an antithetical couplet scribbled on it, and with apparent modesty, he would invite the newcomer to complete the couplet to see whether the man knew something about tonal patterns in classical poetry.

You gain a bit of status that way.

There were a lot more young women living in the valley and Idiot Ren always went down the mountain, on the pretext that he was going to meet some friends, and wouldn't be seen for days on end. Suddenly, he would be gone; suddenly, he would be back, no one knew when. His vegetable garden was overgrown, the weeds so tall a pig could hide there. When he came back, he always brought with him some fancy playthings — a glass bottle, a broken barn lantern, an elastic band, an old newspaper, or a small photograph of somebody or other. As he strutted about in a pair of over-sized leather shoes, the clack-clack of the shoes added to his air of familiarity with new-fangled ways.

Idiot Ren's father, Zhongman, was a tailor who knew nothing about growing vegetables or feeding pigs. He found his son's leather shoes an offensive sight. "You swine! Why the hell do you keep slinking off like that? I'll chop your feet off one of these days."

"You might as well chop off my head. I'll seek reincarnation in Qianjiaping."

"Qianjiaping! You think you'll eat gold and shit silver there?"

"Mr Wang of Qianjiaping wears leather shoes with iron cleats, they make a fine clatter when he walks. Have you watched anything like that?"

Zhongman was reduced to silence, never having seen any leather shoes with iron cleats. It was a good while before he snapped back, "You can't climb a slope or walk in water in leather shoes; besides, they don't let in any air, you only get smelly feet wearing them. What's so great about them?"

"I'm talking about the iron cleats, not the shoes."

"Only mules and horses wear iron for shoes. You want to be an animal too?"

Feeling that his father had insulted his comrade, Idiot Ren flew into a rage and growled at his father vindictively, "Your chili seedlings have all dried up. Bet you didn't know."

Wham! — the tailor hurled a shoe at Idiot Ren, hitting him smack on the head. He would not tolerate such blatant lack of respect from his son.

"Humph!"

Idiot Ren was scared but he refused to rub his head. He went off in a huff into another room to work on the shade of his old barn lantern.

On hearing that Idiot Ren's father had let fly at him, the lads came to find out why. Idiot Ren denied it flatly and changed the subject in all seriousness, "This damn place! It's too conservative."

The lads didn't understand the meaning of "conservative", and so the word shot up in value; and so did Idiot Ren. He was often seen in his room busy with this and that, engrossed in one thing or another. Sometimes it was the antithetical couplets, sometimes the elastic band, and sometimes the making of limekilns. Once he even announced mysteriously to the lads that at Qianjiaping he had learnt how to mine coal and he was now going to dig for gold in the mountains. Yes, gold! Glittering gold! And he did disappear into the mountain for some time with a shovel. A few lads who wanted to benefit from his find spied on him for several days, only to discover that he never did any real digging.

His way of dealing with his companions' doubts was to favour them with a tolerant smile, a pat on the shoulder, and a few encouraging words: "This is the beginning, haven't you heard? Someone has come from the county, he's in Qianjiaping now. Take my word for it." Or he would say, "This is the beginning, take my word. It'll snow tomorrow, and there's no saving the seedlings." And then he would look over his shoulder, as if there was always some invisible man hot on his heels.

And sometimes he would simply say, "Just you wait, maybe tomorrow."

These remarks impressed his friends and won their admiration, but they couldn't figure out what he meant. Something was going to "begin", that's good, of course, but what was he referring to? Was he going to build a limekiln? Or dig gold? Or was he going to leave the mountain, as he'd once said he would, and find a family that would take him in as their adopted son-in-law?[3] But dazzled by his big leather shoes and his meditative look, everyone thought he must be busy at something or other and no one dared trouble him when they needed help for mundane jobs like ploughing fields or felling trees.

Today, a council was held in the temple to discuss the details of an offering to the rice god — a custom Idiot Ren frowned upon. He had seen the folks of Qianjiaping perform the spring ritual; now that was a real offering. But look at this god-forsaken place. Here the fields were ploughed only once a year, the land wasn't properly tilled, and irrigation was poor. How the hell could you grow anything? But then what did he care whether there were crops in the fields, that had nothing to do with his grand plans. Nevertheless, he went to the temple to have a look and saw his father kneeling just like the others before the altar. He sneered. How ridiculous!

---

[3] A person who marries into and lives with his bride's family is the adopted son-in-law of the bride's father. The adopted son-in-law also takes up his bride's family name.

Why didn't they touch their caps in salute? He'd seen people saluting in Qianjiaping.

Brimming with self-confidence, he said to the lad beside him, "It will begin soon."

"Oh, yes." The bemused lad nodded vaguely.

Feeling that no one understood him, Idiot Ren was crestfallen. He turned his gaze to the women to his left. Among them was a married woman who kept wiping the sweat on her face with her sleeve, her ear-rings swaying as she bent towards the sleeve. She, too, was kneeling; the side-seams of her trousers had split, exposing the soft white flesh, but she wasn't aware of it. Idiot Ren squinted, he couldn't see clearly, but it was good enough for his imagination to do the rest. Like a snake, his gaze crept into the trousers through the narrow gap, spiralled nimbly round the curves, and leapt freely up and down the soft smooth surface. In his mind, he had already started to kiss the woman — her shoulders, kneecaps, even her toes, one after another; and he could feel a sour, salty taste on the tip of his tongue ....

He had to talk to that woman about the salute.

4

The women liked to visit each other. They would sidle along beneath the eaves and slip into X or Y's house, and there they would swap news and gossip. They went on and on, until a few kettles of tea had gone down their throats and the level of the urine bucket had risen a few inches, until their faces grew pale and they broke out in gooseflesh. Then they would take their bamboo baskets or their wooden washing clubs, and go their separate ways. For some time they had been going over the story that so and so had a cock which quacked like a duck and that something was not quite right because the New Year was just round the corner and it hadn't snowed at all this month. And Young Bing's mother, just returned from Cock's Tail Village on the other side of the mountain, where she had gone to deliver a baby, brought back the news that Third Grandpa of Cock's Tail had been bitten by a huge centipede at home and died, but no one learnt about it until two days later, by which time one of his feet had been half eaten away by rats. All bad omens, it seemed.

But later on someone else said that Third Grandpa was still alive, for he was seen gathering bamboo shoots on the slopes a few days ago. And so Third Grandpa seemed there and yet not there, his very existence open to question.

As if to bear out the omens, spring was vile, there was a hailstorm, and the rice seedlings turned into icy black mush in the fields, while the few miserable ones left standing looked like chicken feathers waiting to be plucked. This was followed by days of scorching heat, and insects swarmed in the fields.

It so happened that in recent years the birth rate in the village had been high, and every housewife found there was so little rice in the rice-urn that it was all too easy to scrape bottom. Some started to borrow grain and this sparked off a chain reaction — everyone started to borrow in earnest, whether she needed it or not, just to show that she, too, knew how to take advantage of her neighbours. Young Bing's mother also borrowed as if her life depended on it, though she was not too worried. For the past two years, she had been playing the good woman to the hilt, and had offered to look after the ancestral temple. She had kept a cat there, lest the rats should nibble away at the clan records and disturb the ancestors' peace. The cat must be treated well, and so every year two hundred pounds of grain from the communal plot were set aside for it. Every day, Young Bing's mother swaggered down the street carrying a clay pot half filled with rice, calling out to her neighbours that she was going to feed the cat. As soon as she stepped into the temple, she gobbled up the rice herself. Well, that one cat could more or less keep mother and son alive, couldn't it? The villagers seemed to have seen through her ploy and some pointed an accusing finger at her back, but she just frowned and looked defiant, and pretended to hear nothing.

The villagers went on borrowing until there was panic in the air, and the women again started to talk about making offerings to the rice god. This raised Young Bing's mother's spirits, and she threw herself enthusiastically into the discussion. When she had time, she would pick up needle and thread and a shoe sole, take Young Bing by the hand and, her short stout body swaying from side to side, she would drop in on one family after another, hauling her heavy buttocks across the high threshold of every household. To those young women who had never heard of the rice god, she would explain patiently, "It's an old custom, you see. A man must be killed — the one with the thickest hair, and his flesh will be carved up and fed to the dogs. The family whose man is to be sacrificed is known as the family that 'eats the year's bounty' ...." She went on and on, until the women huddled closer and closer together, their eyes starting out of their sockets. At this, she grinned mysteriously and whispered, "Don't worry, your family won't be 'eating the year's bounty'. Your man has thin hair and only a scraggy beard .... Well, not *that* thin ...." Or she would say, "Don't worry, your family won't be 'eating the year's bounty'. Your man Zhu is skinny ..., not much flesh on him .... But then again, he's not *that* skinny .... H'm, H'm."

An intimidating look in her eyes, she comforted the women of one household after another till they were eaten up with fear and anxiety. Then with a crooked finger, she gathered up the tea leaves in her bowl, chewed them noisily, rose from her seat, pulling Young Bing up with her, and bade them farewell in all seriousness, "I'll go and have a watch."

The expression, "Have a watch", was loaded with ambiguity. It could mean "I'll try and find out", or "I'll intercede for you", or "I can see to it for you", or even "I'll go and take a look" — at the chicken coops or what not. But, having been frightened out of their wits, the women warmed to this sort of ambiguity and drew hope and assurance from it.

She went, in fact, to look at the chicken coops.

On the other side of the coops was the house where Idiot Ren and his father lived. When she had seen to the coops, she always turned her head in the direction of the house and darted a glance at it. Her glance was also loaded with ambiguity; it could be interpreted as a greeting, a warning, an attempt to ferret out a secret, or a defiant look of provocation. Every day she stole glances at the house like that a few times, which gave Tailor Zhongman the creeps.

Tailor Zhongman hated women, especially Young Bing's mother. Come to think of it she was actually his sister-in-law and his neighbour. His plot of land stood next to hers and the shade of their trees overlapped in parts. If the dividing wall had been taken down, each would realize that the other also ate, slept, and lectured the children. There wasn't that much difference between them. But the nearer they were, the more closely they could observe each other, and they noticed some differences. Young Bing's mother always hung her clothes to dry on a bamboo pole in a conspicuous spot in her courtyard. The Tailor would be greeted by the sight of women's clothes as he came out of his front door. This brings bad luck, the Tailor thought. That's no way to treat your neighbour! In the courtyard, too, the woman always dried the afterbirth gathered from her midwifery, to use as a tonic for herself or for sale. Those disgusting flesh sacs that had come straight from the wombs of women smelt of blood and were turned this way or that on the mat until they were dry and crinkled. They looked like ghosts straight out of a nightmare, and sent the shivers up your spine. But all this was nothing compared to the look in her eyes. It seemed vacant, pointless and yet pointed, indifferent and yet solicitous, like an invisible venomous snake thrown in your direction.

"She-devil!" The Tailor cursed from his front door one day.

There was no one else in the courtyard. Young Bing's mother, sitting with the ankle of one leg resting on the knee of the other and picking at the calluses on her toes, knew at once who the curses were meant for. Snorting, she tore off two hunks of a callus.

And so they became enemies. But Tailor Zhongman did not take it out on Young Bing. Once, the little old man came timidly to his house, studied the Tailor's pockmarked face, and smeared a length of dress material laid out on a wooden bench with green snot. But the Tailor just glowered at him, and then snatched up the dress material and threw it into the fire.

Keep women and children at arm's length — that's what a true gentleman should do. Whether or not Tailor Zhongman was a true gentleman was hard to say. But he was certainly someone whose word "carried weight" in the village. The expression also embodied an ambiguous concept, and newcomers couldn't figure out what it meant even after they had been in the village some time. It seemed that if you had money, a special skill, a beard, or a son or son-in-law who had made good, your word "carried weight". The lads spent their entire life trying to gain "weight".

The phrase implied that people would come and listen to what you had to say. Tailor Zhongman knew the rudiments of reading; he had been living alone since the early death of his wife, and having read a few tattered thread-bound books left by his sixth uncle, he had learnt quite a lot about the past — history or hearsay — and about historical and mythical figures like Chong Er, a feudal prince of the Spring and Autumn Period, Lu Dongbin, the Taoist god, Ma Yuan, the famous Han general, and the great statesman, Zhuge Liang — his idol. Sometimes, sitting beside the fire and puffing at his gurgling water pipe, he would tell the lads a few of these stories. He did it leisurely, punctuating the story with pauses, breaking off rhythmically after every few words. He often stopped in mid-sentence, heaved a sigh, and then went on with the story. There was always a dazed look in his eyes, as if he was not addressing his audience but speaking to the dead. The lads sat there staring at his stern pockmarked face, and dared not urge him to get on with it.

"What the f___ is so great about motor cars?" He sneered, "Our wise master Zhuge Liang invented the mechanical wooden horse long ago. But the art was lost because those who came after him were idiots."

He went on, "Our ancestors were big and strong. Eight foot tall, and strong enough to lift tens of tons. Not like now, when you get bastards the size of a midget."

Everyone knew he was referring to Young Bing.

The more he sighed and lamented, the more disgruntled he was with life. He fanned himself, but he was still hot and flustered, and felt the sweat break out on the tip of his nose. Damn! It was never so hot in the old days. He swore, too, at his chair for creaking in such a sinister way. Damn! The workmanship nowadays just wasn't up to scratch. In the past, a chair would last from the day of your marriage until you became a grandmother and still remain hard and sturdy .... The more he chewed over the past, the more worried he was that without the wise and learned master Zhuge Liang, the manners and morals of the time would go from bad to worse; he was worried, too, that Cock's Head Village would soon come to a sad end.

And would it?

Right now, everyone was talking about making an offering to the rice god. He sat at home wondering what he should do. Something seemed to have gone wrong. He pondered upon it and in the end realized he was hungry. Lately, very few villagers brought him home with them to make clothes, so he had to cook for himself. Even when they did, the rice they provided was soggy, and this was something he couldn't put up with. If the rice they served wasn't hard like grains of iron, he wouldn't even pick up his chopsticks.

"Ren! Hey, you cripple!" He shouted.

There was no answer.

He shouted again but thought better of it and went upstairs to look for him. He found that his son's bedding, mosquito net, and things like his rusty barn lantern had all gone. Only an empty bed and a few large earthenware jars used for pickling vegetables were left behind. Pickled vegetables had long run out and the jars stood upside down in the corner, like prisoners hung by their heels. Then there was also a coffin — the Tailor had no idea for whom the idiot had it made — lying arrogantly in the middle of the room, snoring.

The Tailor realized that something had happened; he didn't say a word.

The sight of a rat flashing past the foot of the wall made him realize something else. The devil! Yes, this was the devil he'd seen in his dream. In it, this devil-rat was standing on its hind legs with its forepaws cupped before its chest in a gesture of greeting, grinning sympathetically at him. The beast had pink ears, pink feet and blood-shot eyes. That was 'cause it had eaten some rouge on the sly — wasn't that what the books said? If the beast fell into the hands of an evil woman, she could turn it into a dangerous love potion. Damn! Ren the cripple must have been bewitched by this rat. And that was also why the village was doomed!

Swearing and cursing, the Tailor struck at the rat with an iron ruler and shattered a jar, but the rat's tail had disappeared into a crevice in the wall. He dashed into the next room, prised open a wooden cabinet and jabbed holes into two bamboo baskets, but the rat got away. He scuttled down the stairs and made a racket poking and striking at every suspicious spot. In no time, bowls were smashed to pieces and the water jug was knocked over, while the table, chairs and benches were left crouching or kneeling on the floor, leaning askew, swaying, or about to collapse. He started a fire to smoke out the rat and the greasy bed-curtain caught fire and went up in flames.

He managed to wipe out the brutes, six of them in all, large and small. He chopped off their heads and limbs before throwing them into the fire. As the stench rose from the fire, he heard shuffling feet in the courtyard outside. When he turned round to look, he again caught sight of Young Bing's mother looking casually in his direction. This made his blood boil. He gnashed his teeth, poured the rats' ashes into a glass of water and drank it in one gulp.

He turned black in the face and sat down, feeling weak and spent. After a while, he left the house.

It was noon and the cocks were crowing. But it was so quiet in the village it seemed as if no one was there, as if the place had died. Mount Cock loomed above the village. Below its peak — Cock's Head — there was a jagged cliff with multi-coloured veins in the rocks. Some of the rocks looked like swords and spears, others like banners and battle drums; some were like helmets and parts of a suit of armour, others like steeds and chariots. The rocks had something in them, he knew not what, something dark red. He looked up, and it was as if blood was cascading from the mountain top straight onto his face, embroiling him in a tragic battle scene. The Tailor felt it was his ancestors calling him.

The smiling face of an old man appeared from behind a melon trellis by the roadside.

"Have you had lunch, Zhongman?"

"Yes." He answered with a weak smile.

"Going to make an offering to the rice god?"

"Yes."

"Whose head will it be?"

"They say .... Going to draw lots."

"Draw lots?"

"Have you had lunch?"

"Yes."

"I see."

They fell silent.

Beyond the tea groves was the forest. Here, the trees were as tall as the sky. Some of them had thin bamboo strips tied round their trunks to mark them out for coffins. The villagers would, when they were young and strong, come up the mountain to select a tree for their coffins and leave a mark on it. Then they would come back to inspect it once or twice every year. But Tailor Zhongman seldom came into the mountains and had not bothered to pick out a tree. In fact he hated these damned trees for their evil intent. A gentleman does things the proper way: there's a proper way to sit, a proper way to stand, even a proper way to die; he mustn't lose his dignity when he dies. When you die, you die, why all these preparations? He'd come with a knife. He'd pick a tree, lop off the branches, sharpen the stump into a piercing stake, and end his life by throwing himself onto the stake. It'd be a glorious death. He'd met people who had died like that. One of them was Cripple Long over at Mazidong, who died a few years ago. The man had a bad cough, his patience ran out, and he went and killed himself. After his death, it was found that he had raked the soil in front of the stake into a criss-cross of loose earth with his fingers. You could tell it had been a painful death, a glorious death. The event had made it into the clan records.

He picked out a small pine tree and started to chop off its branches clumsily with his tailor's hands.

5

They had wanted to offer up Young Bing's head as a sacrifice to the rice god. To take the life of this useless blockhead was in fact to do him a good turn. He would be spared the pain of having his ears boxed, and he would no longer be a torment to his mother. But when the cleaver was raised, there was a clap of thunder. And everyone started to wonder: was the rice god angry because it was such a meagre sacrifice?

It's hard to know the will of Heaven. So they prepared meat and drink and sought help from a sorcerer. His view was that harvests were bad because Crowing Cock Demon was making trouble. Look at Mount Cock over there and its peak, Cock's Head. The demon was pecking at two strips of land in your village and had gobbled up all your crops.

The villagers started talking at once about blowing up Cock's Head. This involved Cock's Tail Village, which was also a large settlement, with an impressive granite memorial arch at the entrance. A few hundred villagers lived there, the majority grew opium for a living and were quite prosperous. The place had bred a number of scholars, some were said to have become famous writers, and some were holding influential positions in army units in Xinjiang. When they came back to visit their families, they usually arrived in style — in sedan chairs carried by eight burly fellows. For the New Year festivities, every household in the village would slaughter a cow to celebrate. And so the cattle-hide merchants were also drawn there. At the village entrance there was a well and a large camphor tree. Kids often gathered under that tree to play at some sort of chess game with pebbles. The villagers had always regarded the tree and the well as fertility symbols and worshipped them regularly by burning joss sticks and incense, in the hope that more boys would be born in the village. One year, several girls were born in succession and one woman produced a mole, and the atmosphere in the village grew tense as people tried to find out why. After some time, it was said that things had gone wrong because a lad from Cock's Head Village, on passing through, had climbed the camphor tree to gather some birds' eggs, and had broken a branch.

From then on there was enmity between the two villages. Later on, another story went the rounds: Mazidong, which had a family feud with Cock's Tail village, had stirred up trouble on the sly and pinned the blame on Cock's Head Village. But no hard evidence could be found, and the case was left to fizzle out by itself. Even the authorities would not intervene in the affairs of these remote villages. An official did make a trip here once, but only to exact corvee for building a road.

When the folks in Cock's Tail Village were sure that Cock's Head Village was going to blow up Cock's Head, they were furious. The Cock's droppings had kept their soil rich, how could they let anyone destroy Cock's Head? The two parties exchanged bitter words on the mountain a few days ago, the row had ended in a scuffle, and the lads from Cock's Head Village retreated.

But now the village was still very quiet. Cocks crowed, cow-bells tinkled, and from one of the houses came the sound of a woman swearing at her man, though the words were at once absorbed into the heavy pervasive silence. Young Bing stumped along, striking a small brass gong. His pocket was stuffed with sweet potato shreds; he fished out a few, dropping almost as many, and attracted two dogs. They followed him about, weaving in and out between his legs. He grinned knowingly at Tailor Zhongman's mangy black dog and howled at some banana trees. Lately, he had taken a liking to the ancestral temple — he probably hadn't forgotten the big meal he had there the day his head was due to be chopped off. So he pressed forward and, rocking and swaying, made his final "sprint" in that direction.

The children playing in front of the temple caught sight of him.

"Watch, here comes Young Bing."

"*Qu* has no uncle, *qu* is a bastard."

"I know what, *qu* is a spider-man."

"No, *qu*'s mum is a spider-man."

"Let's make *qu* kowtow to us, shall we?"

"No! Make *qu* eat cow dung! The smelliest pile! Ooh! This lump really stinks!"

"Ha, ha! "

....

Young Bing beat the gong, licked the snot running down his
nose, and greeted them excitedly, "Papa —"

"Bah! Who's your papa? Kneel down!"

The kids crowded round him, held him by the ears and forced
him to kneel before a pile of cow-dung. Then they pressed his head
down until his nose almost touched the mucky heap.

Luckily for Young Bing, a group of grown-ups was coming
towards the temple and there was quite a bustle. The kids' attention
was diverted and they broke up reluctantly, leaving Young Bing
kneeling before the cow-dung. When Young Bing finally realized
that the kids had gone, he scrambled up to his feet, muttering,
looking furtively about him. Then he stamped viciously on the
bamboo hat one kid had left behind. After that, he joined the adults
as if nothing had happened, and craned his neck to see what was
going on.

The villagers had brought an ox with them. Its body had been
scrubbed clean, its hair washed to a sheen, and its hipbones stood
out clearly. Its mouth looked wet as usual, and as it stood there
chewing the cud, you could smell the odour of cud rising from its
stomach. But Young Bing wasn't afraid, he was not afraid of animals.

A big man carrying a big hatchet came up. He jabbed the
hatchet into the earth, stripped the upper half of his body naked,
picked up a large bowl of wine, and gulped it down. Young Bing
was fascinated by the hatchet. Its glistening silvery cutting edge,
sharpened and wiped clean, was so smooth, so cool, and so refresh-
ing you wanted to touch it. Its carved wooden hilt had been polished
with tung oil and seemed to fit the grip perfectly. It looked as if it
would fly into your hand any moment and, without your exerting
any strength, slice through the air with a swish and come flashing
down on something.

The man had finished drinking; he threw down the bowl,
smashing it to pieces. Then he snatched up the hatchet, stamped

his feet, let out a grunt, raised his arm and struck. The earth shook and the mountains trembled as the ox's head was severed from its body and then fell slowly to the ground like a lump of earth. Its horns hit the soil, sending heaps of mud flying. Its neck looked like a cut water melon, skin on the outside, flesh and blood on the inside. But the headless body of the ox remained standing for a while.

The children were stunned, they had no idea this was a prediction of their village's fortunes in the coming battle. In the old days, when General Ma Yuan marched south to tame the barbarians, an ox would be beheaded before each battle. If the ox fell forward, it meant victory; otherwise, it was a sign of defeat.

"Victory!"

"Victory for us!"

"Down with f ___ing Cock's Tail!"

A thunderous cheer went up as the ox fell forward. The sound was too loud, too sudden, and smelled too strongly of alcohol; Young Bing was frightened, his upper lip twitched and he started to mutter.

He saw a thread of something red streaming towards him from under the grown-ups' feet. It looked like a slithering crimson snake. He squatted down and felt it with his fingers. It was slimy. He rubbed it on his clothes — that looked nice! Soon, his face and body were stained with ox blood. The blood probably tasted a bit strong as it trickled into his mouth, and the little old man rolled his eyes.

The kids looked at his face and burst out laughing, clapping their hands. He had no idea why they were laughing, but he also laughed.

More people were arriving and there was quite a hubbub. Young Bing's mother had also turned up, a basket in her hand, keen to know how the meat was to be divided. When she heard that those who weren't going to fight wouldn't get a share of the meat, she pouted. On seeing what a fine sight Young Bing was, her face grew bloated with anger. "What the hell have you done to yourself?" She rushed at him and grabbed hold of his mouth, pulling so hard that his eyelids drooped and his eyeballs could not move, but still he seemed to be gazing in the direction of the temple.

"F___ Mama."

"Now I'll have to clean you up. You'll be the death of me, you idiot! You'll drive me to my death!"

"F___ Mama."

Amused by the sight of a son swearing at his mother, a few lads cheered and applauded, filling the air with alcoholic breath, "Well done! Young Bing." "Go on, Young Bing!" "Go on!" .... At this, Young Bing's mother shook with rage, her ugly, ferocious face went all shades of red, and for a long while she couldn't look anybody in the face.

She dragged Young Bing home, pulling him along as if he was a dog and, needless to say, gave him a sound beating. "What the hell did you go out for? They're going to fight, can you fight?"

She tied Young Bing to the chair with a rope, picked up three joss sticks, closed the door and hurried to the temple.

Young Bing fell asleep in the chair. When he woke up, he heard the clang of gongs in the distance, then he heard the blaring of ox horns, and then there was silence. Later on, he had no idea what time it was, he heard a flurrry of scurrying footsteps outside, people yelling, and sharp metallic clangs. Soon afterwards, he heard the wailing of the women .... Something was happening outside.

In the evening, amidst glimmering pine torches, the villagers gathered at the temple, inside and out. All were wearing white headbands, men and women, young and old. At a glance, the place seemed dotted with white specks that rose and fell, drifting and floating in the air. The women were supporting each other, leaning against each other, or hugging each other; they wept disconsolately, beating their chests, stamping their feet, plunging heaven and earth into dark mournful misery, their sleeves and shoulders wet with tears. Young Bing's mother also cried to keep the other women company; her eyes were red and she looked like an innocent child as she dabbed the corners of her eyes with her sleeve every now and then. She was sitting beside Ermen's wife. Holding her by the hand, she sniffed and said in her outsider's accent, "That's life! It's the same with plants. If it's time to go, you go. You must take it bravely. You still have your sons. But what about me? I've no idea whether my man is alive or dead, and Young Bing is no use!"

She said it in all sincerity, but the women went on weeping.

"When you go and fight, somebody will get killed. What does it matter whether you die early or late? Death comes to us all sooner or later. If you die early, you get an early reincarnation, you may even be born into a rich family and find your lot improved, who knows."

The women still sobbed and wailed in all their different voices.

Young Bing's mother was probably thinking back over some painful memories — she beat her thighs and burst into tears, and the tail of the white headband draped over her chest rose and fell. "Mama and Papa! How cruel you've been to me! You loved eldest sister, second sister and third sister, but never me! Oh! How cruel you were! Not even a night pot or a wash basin ...."

The light was growing brighter and stronger. The villagers had formed themselves into a ring and set up in their midst a tall, make-shift kitchen range, on top of which sat a big iron pot. The mouth of the pot was well above eye-level, but it was obvious something was boiling and bubbling inside the pot. The hot billowing steam threw the bats on the beams into panic and they were fleeing in all directions. The grown-ups all knew that a pig and an enemy's corpse had been carved up and thrown into the pot. A man climbed up a sturdy ladder, lifted a bamboo spear longer than a carrying pole, and jabbed it into the pot. Whatever he speared out he then distributed to the villagers, young and old, men and women. You didn't have to know what you were eating, you simply ate it. If you said no, someone would drag you out and force you to kneel before the iron pot, and then poke you in the mouth with the bamboo spear. This was called "eating meat from the spear".

The firewood crackled, the pine rosin popped, and billowing steam surged from the pot. Those near the fire felt the heat in their crotches and drew back instinctively. The long oily bamboo spear gleamed in the light of the fire; even the juice which now and then dripped from it seemed bright and shiny, like fire beads sinking into the dark. A burly fellow stripped to the waist suddenly leapt to his feet and screamed like a mad man, "Those who fear death, stand aside! I alone ..." But he was held back by several pairs of hands. Below every strip of white cloth a pair of fiery eyes sparked. You'd better not look at the walls or the ceiling, or else you'd see shadows many times larger than life size, even dozens of times larger, now stretched out, now crushed and flattened, huge one moment, dwarfed the next, their silhouettes contorted at random into all weird shapes.

"Delong's wife, come here!"

Young Bing's mother's name was called. Her eyes were blurred with tears, and she was still beating her knees.

"I don't want it ..."

"Bring your bowl here."

"It's human flesh ..."

"You eat it, Young Bing."

Young Bing, biting on the cord of his open-crotch pants and looking annoyed, was pushed to the front. He grabbed a piece of some sort of lung and stuck it into his mouth; but it didn't taste nice, for he showed the whites of his eyes and staggered anxiously back into his mother's arms.

"Eat it!" Someone yelled.

"Eat it!" Many voices urged him.

An old man pointed a finger with a fingernail over an inch long at Young Bing, then coughed loudly to clear his throat and lectured him, his voice quivering with emotion, "We must all hate our enemy and we must live and die together. You're a son of Cock's Head clan, how can you not eat it?"

"Eat it!" The man holding the bamboo spear thrust the bowl at Young Bing. And the huge looming shadow of a hand appeared on the ceiling.

6

Idiot Ren thought that the clap of thunder that split the sky the other day was probably a sign of heaven's displeasure with his lascivious thoughts. He rolled up his bedding and left the mountain, his heart in his mouth, partly to flee from the thunder god's fury, and partly because he wanted to look for some odd jobs until he could find a family that would take him in as their adopted son-in-law. On his way down the mountain, he heard that a troop of riflemen had passed through Qianjiaping not so long ago and he was delighted with the news. Ha! Wasn't this the beginning?! But although it was true the riflemen had passed through Qianjiaping, they didn't go to Cock's Head Village, nor did they invite him for any sort of chat. How disappointing! He met instead a fellow who carried coal and who had just come out of the mountains. The man told him that Cock's Head had been fighting with Cock's Tail and that a corpse had floated down Mazi Stream, and for some reason its feet were sticking out of the water. It was a scary sight ....

Idiot Ren remembered his two close friends in Cock's Tail — one a kiln master, the other a teacher. Perhaps he should go home and persuade his people to patch up their quarrel with the Cock's Tail folks. After all they drank from the same stream, what good was there in fighting? Let them come together and have a meat meal and everything could be straightened out.

Idiot Ren arrived home to find his father lying in bed and seriously wounded — the day the Tailor had tried to end his life with the stake, he had been saved and brought home by a man gathering firewood in the forest.

"*Qu* is an ungrateful son, or else Zhongman wouldn't have taken such a desperate step."

"Although Zhongman has been saved this time, sooner or later the poor man will die of a broken-heart."

"It's hard being a father, hard indeed."

"Just look at *qu*'s features. See how *qu*'s brows and eyes droop. *Qu*'s the sort that'll bring bad luck to *qu*'s parents."

"*Qu*'s mother died early, mayhap ...."

These words glided through the air from behind him and bore their way into his ears, but Idiot Ren pretended not to hear. Aimlessly he swept the floor, aimlessly he trampled on a few ants. Then he took a few puffs at his father's water pipe and after that, he went to the temple.

A bunch of people had gathered outside the temple discussing the feud. It seemed a god-sent opportunity to improve his tarnished image.

"Well, maybe there's no need to blow up Cock's Head". Assuming the air of a well-mannered and impartial scholar, he analysed the situation for them slowly and condescendingly, "If you can't blow it up, then keep out of its way. But then, well, to be fair, to be absolutely fair, that f___ing Cock's Tail (he was quick to follow the others in calling Cock's Tail Village 'f___ing Cock's Tail') came striking their gongs and brandishing their spears, they've really gone too far! And yet there's no point fighting over trifling matters, no point really —" He closed his eyes and drawled this out, and then he looked up and swept his audience with a ferocious glance, "But we have to make a good showing, have to show them we won't be bullied!"

The righteousness of the feud was explained by him in a novel and heroic way. No one paid much attention to what he had said, but all were impressed by his ferocious glare. Sensing this as he watched them through narrowed eyes, he got even more carried away. He tore open his jacket, snatched up a hoe, jabbed ferociously at the ground and roared, "Revenge! I'll lay down my life — today!"

Fearlessly he tightened his belt, fearlessly he rushed in and out of the temple, fearlessly he scuttled to the latrine. His actions made everyone look at him with respect. When he realized by and by that the ox horn had not sounded today and that there was nothing much he could do, he went home to cook himself some maize gruel.

This really was the beginning, it seemed; for he turned and turned about in and out of the village, and would position himself before a tree or a boulder, and study it, frowning. The lads were so impressed they didn't dare disturb him even when it was his turn to take up duty at the sentry post. When his tour of the village was complete, it was with a heavy heart that he spoke to those he happened to meet.

"Jin, please look after my father for me in the days to come. We've been like brothers from the same family since we were young, and we've always shared everything. That time when we went to chase meat — I'd have lost my life if it hadn't been for you. I'll always remember your kindness ...."

"Second Uncle, do you still get those nagging pains in your back? Please take care of yourself. Certain things ... I'm to blame. I'd wanted to gather some firewood for you and stock it up in the hut, but .... That time when I repaired the floorboards for you, I didn't do a good job. In future, help yourself to some good food when you want to. Wear some good clothes when you want to. And don't work in the fields if your bones are stiff. Your worthless nephew won't be able to look after you for long. Please keep these words in your heart ...."

"Huang, my sister, there's something I want to tell you. I've done a lot of stupid things in the past, I hope you won't hold them against me. I once stole two melons from your garden and served them up for the kiln master, you didn't know that. It hurts me to think of it now. I've come specially to apologize to you, to beg your forgiveness. Curse me if you want to ...."

"Yao, ... are you, ... are you doing the washing? This time ... I, I really have to go ..., please ..., please don't be sad. I'm a good-for-nothing, I can't fight, and I'm no scholar; I can't even look after my own plot of land. But life is short and death comes to us all. I'm a man, and when home and country calls, I must do my duty, don't you agree? Some things ..., it's hard to explain them now. Anyway, as long as you still care for your brother Shiren, I'll be happy and content. You must ... you must be strong. Things will get better soon. Goodbye now ...."

He had his sorrow under control and only sniffed now and then.

But everyone was touched and there was sadness in the air. "Shiren, our brother, don't talk like this!"

"No, my mind is made up!" He hung his head and stared at a broken tile on the ground.

No one knew what he wanted to do, or what he was going to do. But the quick clack-clack of his leather shoes on the flagstones could still be heard; evidently he had not yet gone and made a martyr of himself. But then so much was going on in the village — hens were found on roof tops, buffaloes were caught eating crops, and Young Bing's mother was always quarrelling with someone over Young Bing — no one had the time to find out what Idiot Ren was up to dashing about here and there. Gradually people got used to his habits; if he wasn't busying himself over this and that, they would even have felt that something was missing, that something was not quite right.

One day, the Tailor shouted his son out of the house. Idiot Ren wiped his face and strode to the temple. The people inside were about to file a complaint to the authorities. But since the villagers had always settled their feuds among themselves and never lodged any complaints with the authorities, no one had the faintest idea about the wording and the form of such a letter. A few elders put their heads together and recalled a term once used by Tailor Zhongman. At once they said to the man with the writing brush, "Mayhap we should call it a supplication?"

Idiot Ren's bristling hair rose above the crowd and, waving his hand in disagreement, said, "No, no. It's called a report."

"'Supplication' sounds better, no?"

"No, 'report' is better."

"We must show a proper respect to the authorities."

"The best way of showing our respect is to call it a report." Idiot Ren smiled tolerantly, "I know it for sure, I do."

"Go ask your uncle."

"What he knows is completely out of date."

"It's called a supplication."

"Don't you know that times have changed?"

"A report? It sounds blunt. Those down there may be using this term, I know. But of course you think that even their farts smell better."

"Trust me and you won't go wrong, my dear uncles and brothers. There was a heavy downpour yesterday, shouldn't the old customs be swept away? We're too conservative here! Yes, we are. Go to Qianjiaping and have a watch. Because they all use soya sauce, therefore they use the term 'report'. Don't you understand? Do you know what elastic bands are made of? They're made of rubber and a good thing it is, rubber. Just think, can we still file what you call a supplication? And precisely because of that, we have to make up our minds quickly. There is no time to lose. So put your heads together and think."

His volley of "because", "therefore", "precisely" and "so" had totally confused the villagers and for a good while, they were at a loss for words. Then they remembered that there had indeed been a heavy downpour yesterday, and so they yielded to his rhetoric and solemnity and reluctantly agreed to draft a "report-supplication".

More problems cropped up. The elders preferred to use classical Chinese while he favoured the vernacular; the elders would rather stick to the lunar calendar while he advocated the use of what he called "the western calendar"; the elders wanted to affix a hoof-shaped seal to the report, but he dismissed the idea, saying that the hoof-shaped seal was too old-fashioned, too provincial, and that to avoid becoming a laughing stock, they should use "signatures" instead. One moment, he was lost in thought, another moment, he was kind and tolerant, the next moment, he nodded modestly in agreement with the others — only to drag them back to his own line of argument with his "but come to think of it", and to introduce them to all sorts of new ways and methods, thus making himself out to be a liberal-minded advocate of the new school.

"You pockmarked cripple, you've got hairy ears!" Zhuyi's eldest lad suddenly exclaimed.

Idiot Ren tried to laugh it off, shaking his head and squinting even more. He realized that he should not cut himself off from the masses and so he fished out some tobacco leaves and distributed them among the men, leaving none for himself. With this generous gesture, he set the seal on a flawless performance for the day.

He left the temple and went enthusiastically to collect some medicinal herbs for his father. In a moment of carelessness, he stumbled over Young Bing who was sitting on the ground, and nearly fell.

Young Bing had come to watch the fun. Not finding any, he turned to playing with chicken droppings, now and then scratching the running sore on his head. For half the day, he had been in a bad mood and didn't say "papa" even once.

7

They were defeated again and again; again and again heads were lost to the enemies. They panicked, and let their imagination run away with them. A lad suddenly remembered something peculiar. He said that that day when they were about to offer up Young Bing as a sacrifice to the rice god, a clap of thunder had come out of the blue. Afterwards, they had tried to read their fortunes in the battle by killing an ox, but it didn't work. It seemed to have been a bad omen when Young Bing swore, "F___ Mama", and something bad did happen .... Wasn't it strange?

Now that he'd mentioned it, everyone found Young Bing most mysterious. Just think: he could only say "Papa" and "F___ Mama". Could it be that these two expressions are actually the divination symbols for *yin* and *yang*?

They decided to tap this living medium's power of divination. So they quickly took down a door and used it to carry Young Bing to the square outside the temple.

"Bing, our master."

"Bing, our lord."

"Immortal Bing."

The men fell prostrate before him and waited attentively for an answer, deep furrows marking their foreheads as they strained to look at him, their heads bowed.

Young Bing had enjoyed the ride on the door and was beaming, the wrinkles on his face all smoothed out. He stamped on the door that had stopped rocking. When he discovered that it wouldn't move anymore, he rolled his eyes.

They didn't know how to interpret that.

Did he have to be fed before he would show his power? Some-one brought him a rice dumpling and he perked up at once. He grabbed a piece clumsily with his fingers, but it slipped and fell to the ground. It was lying by his right foot, but he had such trouble coordinating the movements of his eyes and his head that he in fact looked to his left. For every piece of dumpling he put into his mouth, there was a piece dropped onto the ground. He would invariably try and look for it, and would invariably turn the wrong direction. When he caught sight of the bits he had dropped earlier on, he picked them up and stuck them into his mouth.

He clapped his hands. A sparrow called, he looked up and rolled his eyes slowly in the wrong direction. Finally, he pointed his finger in a certain direction and mumbled, "Papa."

"Victory!"

The men leapt into the air shouting for joy. But what was he pointing at? What exactly did it mean? Looking in the direction he was pointing at, they saw a corner of the temple and the gentle curving end of the eaves. Blades of grass had crept out from the crevices of the tiled roof; the rafters had rotted and looked worn and charred, like an old wounded phoenix gazing at the sky, weighed down by its heavy long wings. From under the eaves came the chirping of sparrows.

"*Qu* is pointing at the sparrows."

"No, higher, at the eaves."

"'Higher' rhymes with 'retire'. Mayhap we should make it up with them?"

"Nonsense! 'Higher' rhymes with 'fire'. We should attack with fire."

A heated argument developed. Eventually, they bowed to the authority of those whose word "carried weight". And so they launched another attack, using fire this time. When the men returned after a skirmish, they discovered that yet a few more heads were missing in the head-count.

The dogs in the village had got used to the blaring of the ox horns. On hearing it, their fur would bristle, and they would scramble through the doors, leap over stone walls, shoot off like arrows straight at where the horns were sounding, and follow closely upon the heels of the moving figures, their hearts full of hope. On the slopes, at crossroads, or in the gullies, corpses could be found. The dogs would pounce on the corpses, tearing them to pieces, and crunch the bones. They had all grown fat from this. Their eyes blood-shot, they dashed about in the tall grasses. You couldn't see them, all you could see was the grass moving — curving lines like many a grass-dragon on the move. Where the dragons' heads were, there would be blood stains, and lumps of flesh and pieces of bone, and the whole village was littered with the remains of their spoils. Sometimes when you chanced to lift a bundle of firewood in the kitchen, a stranger's hand or foot might suddenly fall onto the ground.

The dogs had grown very interested in humans all of a sudden. When a few villagers gathered together for a discussion, or when people started to quarrel, the dogs would be there at once. They frisked about, waiting for some outcome, their fangs bared, their tongues hanging out like fluttering ribbons, like ripples. It was said that when Zhuyi's grandpa was taking a nap under a tree one day, the dogs pounced on him and bit him, mistaking him for a corpse.

Young Bing shitted on a chair.

As usual, Young Bing's mother called the dogs to lick it up. "Ah — li —, Ah — li —, Ah — li —."

The dogs came, took a sniff and sauntered off. They seemed to have lost interest in human excrement. They came because they had been called, they had to put in an appearance somehow lest they would seem too arrogant to their masters. Life had taken a turn for the better but they didn't forget to whom they owed their loyalty.

And so the village became littered with faeces; flies came in swarms, and the place began to stink.

Young Bing's mother ran into Zhuyi's wife one day. Sniffing, she said, "Why's there this dreadful smell about you?"

The woman glared at her, "That's strange, you're the one who smells."

The two women started to sniff and found that their hands stank, their sleeves stank, and even their wooden washing clubs and bamboo baskets had a dreadful smell. Only then did it dawn on them that there had been a putrid smell in the air for some time. In the last few days, certainly no one had gone to put out the cow-dung and the pig manure and the yards were black and slimy. How could the place not stink?

Young Bing's mother's family was very particular about cleanliness, so she had always kept up some special habits of her own. She got a bundle of straw and some tea dregs, carried Young Bing's soiled pants and the chair to the stream, and rubbed and scrubbed them twice. Still she couldn't get rid of the smell. But she was already exhausted. Her eyes rolled upward involuntarily as she gasped for breath. Although in the past she had taken quite a few cauls and placentas to build up her health, lately, there had been too little food to keep her going. As she struggled to get up, she felt giddy and collapsed on the ground.

She had no idea how she managed to crawl home. Anyway she was lucky not to have been torn to pieces by the dogs. Staring at the fly-covered mosquito net, she broke down in tears and wailed, "Mama and Papa! How cruel you've been to me! You loved eldest sister, second sister, third sister, but never me! Oh! Not even a night pot or a wash basin ...."

Young Bing watched her timidly, then he beat his small brass gong hesitantly, in an apparent effort to please her.

She turned to look at her son and wiped away the snot running from his nose with the palm of her hand. Then she nodded at him kindly, "Come, come and sit beside Mama."

"Papa." The son sat steadily beside her.

"Yes, go and find that heartless devil!"

She clenched her teeth as she spat out the words. Her eyes — black bulging pupils encircled by large rings of white — were like peacock feathers. It was a horrifying sight, Young Bing was stunned.

"F___ Mama!" He said softly, trying to feel out where he stood with her.

"You got to go and look for your papa. He's called Delong. He has faint eyebrows and a small head, and he can sing some stupid songs."

"F___ Mama."

"Remember this, he may be in Chenzhou, or in Yuezhou. Some people have seen him there."

"F___ Mama."

"You must tell that beast how he's made life hell for us! They beat you up everyday, and everyday I'm bullied. The more re-spectable families all treat us like dirt. We'd have long been dead but for the cat meals. But then death would have been a blessing for us! What we have to put up with ..., it's worse than death! Go tell him. Tell him how we suffered!"

"F___ Mama."

"Kill him!"

Young Bing didn't say a word this time. His upper lip twitched.

"H'm, you got my point, you're with me, I know. You're a good boy, Mama's good boy." Young Bing's mother smiled as a tear-drop fell from her eye.

With a vegetable basket in her hand, she staggered slowly up the mountain and never came back again. Later on, all sorts of stories were told about her. Some said she had died from a snake bite, others that the folks of Cock's Tail Village had killed her, yet others said she had run into a demon and lost her way, and had fallen down a cliff .... None of these stories could be proved. But you could know for sure that her body had been devoured by the dogs.

Young Bing waited and waited for Mama to return. The sun had set, the frogs started to croak, and the sound of footsteps on the narrow mountain track in front of the house could no longer be heard, but still there was no sign of that familiar face. The mosquitoes seemed to be on the rampage, and he itched all over from their bites. The little old man scratched so furiously he began to bleed. He lost his temper. He wanted to punish that woman. He stormed into the house, knocked over the chairs, splashed tea onto the bed, and poured ashes into the hanging water jug. Then he picked up a stone and hurled it at the iron pan, smashing it. He had turned the world upside down.

Everything had sunk into darkness, but still there was no familiar shuffle of feet outside the house. Only the moan of the pock-marked tailor rose now and then from the house next door.

The little old man fell asleep with the mosquitoes and insects buzzing round him. Then he woke up, hungry, and stumbled out into the courtyard.

The moon was full. Its gleaming white light had rendered everything as clear as it was in daytime, so clear you felt you could see every tree, every blade of grass on the hill opposite. Where the stream gurgled, there was a rippling sheet of silvery water with a few black shadows here and there, as if holes had been poked in it. They were of course the silhouettes of rocks sitting proudly in the water. The frogs had stopped croaking, they had probably gone to sleep, too. But somewhere in the distance the dogs barked together, as if something had happened.

Young Bing sat in front of the chicken coops, his thumb in his mouth. He thought for a while, then he made his way out of the village.

Mama used to bring him along when she went to deliver babies. Mama could be in those places now. He had to find her.

He walked along the moonlit mountain track, steering his way through heavy rolling mist and clouds; he sauntered along, his body leaning slightly forward and his wobbly knees knocking at every step, as if they might give way and snap any moment. He pressed on, mindless of the time, the distance, until he tripped on a bamboo hat and a rattan shield, and sent them rolling with a rattle. He muttered something, relieved himself, and went on again. There was a human body lying on the ground a little further on; it was a woman, but Young Bing did not know her. He shook her hand, boxed her ears and pulled at her hair, but he couldn't wake her. His hands touched her breasts. Remembering dimly that the fat lump could be a feed, the little old man cupped it in his hands and sucked. When he couldn't draw anything from it, he lost interest. But the woman's body and limbs were soft and springy, so the little old man climbed on her belly, leaned back, pressed forward, and was pleased because his bony buttocks were so comfortably supported.

"Papa." He was tired. Resting his body on the woman that was like Mama, he fell asleep, his head between her breasts. In the moonlight, both faces were papery white, and the ear-rings glistened.

That, too, was a child's mother.

·

8

"Papa."

Young Bing pointed at the gentle curving end of the eaves at one corner of the temple and laughed foolishly.

There was nothing unusual about that corner, it simply looked like an old wounded phoenix. The trees and soil of these mountains had given birth to the phoenix's feathers, for the tiles were baked in the village kilns. Perhaps its feathers were too heavy and it could not fly away, it could only stay here listening to the turtledoves, the partridges, the thrushes and the crows, to the quiet mornings and the equally quiet nights. And so it grew old. But it still held its head high, gazing at a star or a wisp of cloud. It still wanted to soar high into the sky, carrying the whole rooftop with it, like it had done in ancient times, when it had led the ancestors of Cock's Head Village to a better place.

Two lads were coming out of the temple carrying a large cauldron. When they saw Young Bing, they were taken aback.

"Isn't that Young Bing?"

"Hasn't *qu* died?"

"Not *qu*'s turn yet, I suppose. *Qu* was born lucky."

"The Yama[4] has probably forgotten *qu*."

"The bastard. That f___ing sign *qu* sent us the last time nearly did me in!"

Lately, the villagers had taken a dislike to Young Bing. They felt that he had duped them and they even blamed their bitter defeat on him. He had brought them bad luck, and it was because of him that the village was plagued by disasters of all sorts. The two lads put down the cauldron, and when they saw that Young Bing had been sitting on the bamboo hat one of them had left under the tree and had crushed it, they got even madder. One of them stomped up to Young Bing and slapped him on the face. The lad didn't really hit hard, but Young Bing fell like a bundle of straw. The other drew out a sharp knife and poked at the tip of Young Bing's nose, and Young Bing felt a spray of spittle on his face, "Come on, slap your mouth, quick. Or I'll offer you up as a sacrifice to my knife!"

"You dare!" A cold voice rose behind the lad. He turned round and saw a pockmarked face livid with rage.

Tailor Zhongman was most particular about seniority in the clan. He prodded the lads in the forehead with his finger and snarled, "*Qu* is your senior, how dare you be so rude?"

The lads were at once conscious of their position in the clan, conscious that Tailor Zhongman was in fact Young Bing's uncle. They exchanged a look, avoiding the Tailor's eyes, and went to pick

---

[4]King of the Underworld.

up the cauldron.

Tailor Zhongman made his way home. He took a few steps, paused, turned round and held out his hand to his nephew who was sitting on the ground, "Give me your hand!"

Young Bing backed away, his eyes did not seem to be looking at the Tailor but at the tall tree behind the Tailor. Then he tried to suppress his fear and forced a smile, his face contorting, his upper lip twitching. And it was a good while before he gingerly raised his bony hand. The hand was skinny and cold, like the claw of a chicken. The Tailor clutched it and shivered, a burning sensation in the pit of his stomach.

He wiped Young Bing's face, drove away the flies buzzing round Young Bing's head, and fastened a button on Young Bing's coat. He had no idea who had made this coat, he had never made any clothes for Young Bing.

"Come with me!"

"Papa."

"Be a good boy."

"Papa."

"Who's your papa?"

"F___ Mama."

"Beast!"

....

He did not look at Young Bing anymore. Holding him by the hand, he went down the steps in silence. For some strange reason, he suddenly remembered the many clothes he had made, long ones, short ones, big ones, small ones. One after another they drifted towards him, like headless ghosts floating before his eyes. That corpse from Cock's Tail which he saw the other day, hadn't he made the clothes it had on? He recognized the needlework. At this, he clutched Young Bing's hand even more tightly, "Don't be afraid, I'm your papa. Come with me."

There was a type of poisonous weed in the mountains called

"sparrow-taro". It was said that birds that touched it would die at once while beasts that trod on it would be paralysed. Tailor Zhongman had collected a few bunches of the weed and just now he had boiled them to produce half a pot of poisonous liquid. The village had been out of food for three days; the few cows and oxen that remained had to be kept for breeding, while the young men and women had to stay on to beget children and carry on the family name, but surely the old and the weak could go. The records in the temple had it in black and white that their ancestors had done the same thing. Tailor Zhongman had always felt that he had been born at the wrong time and did not have much to show for himself before his ancestors, but today he finally had a chance to keep up the ancient tradition and die for the clan. This was some consolation.

The tailor poured half a bowl down Young Bing's throat before he left the house. A pebbled path zig-zagged up the slope to the village from his place. On both sides of the road, there were low walls built from slabstones, and sturdy timber huts. Dragonflies and bees were fluttering over the flowers and the grass that had shot up from the crevices of the walls. Some villagers who had wanted to build houses here had marked out the sites by the side of the road, or even right across it, and wooden beams and pillars could be seen standing there. Sometimes the villagers would let a few years pass before they put up the walls and the tiles, and passers-by could sit and rest on the wooden frames. If there was a plague or something, pieces of red paper would be pasted onto these empty beams to exorcise the evil spirits.

The Tailor knew where the young and the old, the weak and the sick, lived. He went up to each house with his earthenware jug. The elderly were all waiting for him by the threshold, as if by tacit agreement. On seeing him, they got up, holding on to the door for support or leaning on walking sticks, and nodded knowingly at him.

"Is it time?"

"Yes, are you ready?"

"Yes."

Yuangui, the old herdsman, pleaded, "Zhongman, I want to go and cut some hay for the cow."

The tailor replied, "You go. I can wait."

The old man tottered out to the fields. When he finished cutting the hay, he wrung his hands and came tottering back. He took a china bowl from the tailor and poured the liquid down his throat in two gulps, a few drops still clinging like beads to his beard.

"Have a seat, Zhongman."

"No, I better move on. It's hot and dry today."

"Yes, it is."

Another old man who was rocking a baby in his arms asked the tailor to take a look at the baby and said with tears in his eyes, "Zhongman, don't you think *qu* should put on a new gown? The one you made, it hasn't been worn yet."

The tailor blinked to show that he agreed.

The old man turned and went into the house. After a while, he came out again; the baby had a new gown on, with a longevity chain hung round his neck. The old man's thin shrivelled hand stroke the new gown, making it rustle. "That's better. That's better."

"It fits quite well."

"Babies mess up clothes easily."

The man fed the liquid to the baby first and then took a big gulp himself.

The jug was now very light. The tailor thought for a while and remembered that there was one more senior he had yet to visit — grandma of the Yutang family. The old woman always sat at the door basking in the sun like a door-god. She was so old you could hardly tell whether she was a man or a woman. Her nails were long, her toothless gums always moving up and down to slurp back the saliva dribbling from her mouth. Her skin was like a loose garment draped over a skeleton, and when she crossed one leg over the other, both of them touched the ground. She could not hear what was said to her, and would only glance indifferently at whoever went up to address her. Perhaps in a lot of places one would come across old folks like her — a living symbol of this type of village.

The tailor walked right up to her; only then did she realize that someone was there, and a faint gleam appeared in her cloudy eyes. She, too, seemed to understand. She slurped back the saliva, pointed at the tailor, and then slowly pointed at herself.

The tailor knew what she meant. He went down on his knees and prostrated himself before her, and then poured the black liquid into her toothless mouth.

All these elders sat facing east as they took the liquid. Their ancestors had come from that direction, and they were going to return there. A sea of clouds met their eyes, wave upon wave, all frozen still, motionless. The side illuminated by the sun framed the shadowy parts in snow-white translucence. A few mountains had poked their heads out from the clouds, as if they were feeling lonely and wanted to exchange a few words with one another. An enormous butterfly was fluttering its golden wings over the clouds, like a glistening spark, crossing mountains and ridges that stretched endlessly, until finally it landed on the back of a black bull. It looked like the largest butterfly in the world.

The men from Cock's Tail Village arrived; and soon, women, children and dogs also came in twos and threes. They had heard that the folks on this side would "cross the mountains" and settle elsewhere, and had come to see if they had left behind anything useful. Just the day before, the two villages had had a reconciliation meal and sorted out the business about prisoners and dead bodies. Both had, moreover, broken their swords in an oath, pledging never to take revenge on each other.

The timber huts had burned down one after another and wisps of black smoke were curling up into the air from the sites, bare now except for some broken earthenware jugs and empty stoves. The stoves looked like black greedy mouths as they stood exposed on

the unbelievably narrow plots of land that had once been occupied
by the huts. Had these folks lived their lives within such small
confines? The young men and women had put on their white
headbands, their faces were sallow, like oil lamps, and there was a
flurry of activity as they got ready to set out on the journey — driving
the cattle, tying up ploughs and rakes, packing cotton, pots and
pans, wooden drums, and this and that into baskets big and small.
A rusty barn lantern swung from the back of a cow.

As a farewell ritual, they went and prostrated themselves before
a row of new graves. Then everyone scraped out a lump of earth
and put it inside his jacket. After that they raised their voices in a
chorus, "Hey! Yo! Wei!", and started to sing "*Jian*".

Their forefather was Jiangliang, Jiangliang came after Fufang,
Fufang came after Huoniu, Huoniu came after Younai, and Younai
came after Xingtian. They used to live on the shores of the East Sea.
As the family swelled and the clan grew bigger and bigger, the place
became so crowded there wasn't even an open space the size of a
mat. Five of the women who married into the clan had to share the
use of one pestle room for grinding grain, and there was only one
water bucket to be shared among six unmarried daughters. How
could life go on like that? There wasn't even an open space the size
of a mat! And so they picked up their hoes and rakes and, with
Phoenix leading the way, they crowded into maple-wood boats and
nan-wood boats.

> Grandma led the clan, Oh, from the east afar,
> Grandpa left the east, Oh, a long long line behind,
> On and on they went, Oh, the mountains were so high,
> They turned back to look, Oh, their homes behind the clouds,
> On and on they went, Oh, through a gap in the sky,
> Grandma and grandpa, Oh, their hearts were heavy,
> To the west of them, Oh, the mountains stretched so far,
> The road grew weary, Oh, was the end not near?
> ....

Men and women all sang in earnest, or more appropriately still, they shouted in earnest. They did not always sing in harmony; their voices were dry, harsh, untrained, and without tremolos. They bellowed and shouted, craning their necks and bending forward until they were out of breath; then their voices glided down on a note, then went on with the next phrase. This type of singing reminded you of places with precipitous mountain cliffs, bamboos as tall as the sky, and excessively thick and heavy thresholds. Only such places could bring out such sounds.

And there were ornamental notes, and the refrain — "Hey! Yo! Hey!". Naturally, it was a splendid and magnificent song; it was like the singers' eyes, like the women's ear-rings and bare feet, like the dainty smiling flowers beside their bare feet. There was no trace at all of wars and disasters, and not the slightest hint of bloodshed or violence.

None whatever.

In the distance, the human figures looked like a herd of cattle as they dwindled into black specks. Then they went down a green mountain pass and receded deeper and deeper into the forests. But the tinkling of cow-bells and the sound of people singing continued to seep softly through the green. By contrast, the valley seemed a lot quieter, and the gurgling of the stream grew loud all of a sudden. Beside the stream there were rocks and boulders, masses of them. A few looked markedly different from the rest. Smooth and gleaming, they had served the women in their washing. They looked like dull mirrors, mirrors that had collected a myriad of reflections but would never allow them to see the light of day again. Perhaps when weeds and trees had grown over this stretch of ruins, the wild animals would come here and howl. Hunters and merchants passing through the land would see no difference between this and other mountain passes. Only a few boulders by the side of the stream would look a little unusual — they seemed to carry some sort of history, some sort of secret.

Young Bing had surfaced from no one knew where. Believe it or not, he survived. What was more, the running sore on his head had stopped festering and a scab had formed. He was sitting naked on a low wall and stirring the water in a half-full earthenware jug with a twig, stirring up eddies of reflected sunlight. Listening to the song in the distance, he clumsily clapped his hands once and, mumbling in a very very soft voice, he called again and again the man whose face he had never seen —

"Papa."

Although he was skinny, his navel was the size of a copper coin, and the kids hovering round him stared at him with wonder and amazement, with admiration too. They glanced at that admirable navel and offered him a handful of pebbles, smiling, looking friendly. Then they clapped their hands, like he'd done just now, and shouted,

"Pa Pa Pa Pa Pa!"

A woman came and said to another woman, "Is this big enough for the swill?" And she walked up to Young Bing and took away that half jug of swirling light.

January 1985

Woman Woman Woman

1

Because of her, we had to shout and scream nearly all our life. Yesterday the old woman downstairs popped her head into our room to complain that our kitchen sewer had clogged up again and filthy water was seeping into her place. I shouted "sorry" so loudly she was startled, her pupils drawn instinctively together till she looked almost cross-eyed. I sensed that something was not quite right, but before I knew it, I was roaring for her to come in for a cup of tea or something .... In the end she put on a brave smile, withdrew her head and left.

Oh dear, I was always shouting and screaming, screaming and shouting. At the dining table, into the telephone, or even when I was on the street whispering to my wife the name of a hated acquaintance I had just caught sight of, and especially in front of women with wrinkled faces and necks. As soon as my attention wandered, my throat would tighten all of a sudden, ready to scream or shout. I kept thinking those women were Uncle Yao[1] and that I

------

[1] "Yao" means "the youngest".

had to greet them or send them away at the top of my voice. It made my days rather tense.

But none of them was Uncle Yao.

Uncle Yao was in fact Aunt Yao, my youngest aunt. In my home village, women were addressed by male titles. I'd no idea whether it was done out of respect or disrespect, or whether this might not cause some problems, just as I had no idea how it would affect me now that Aunt Yao was no longer by my side. It'd been two years already, two long, endless years, the world ought to have quieted down, and I shouldn't have had to scream and shout anymore. But I was beginning to suspect that my hearing was deteriorating and that the membranes in my ears, grown hard like a layer of rock, were filtering out all the sounds so that they only reached me in a timid whisper. Was that how Aunt Yao went deaf? The story had it that her father, too, was hard of hearing. Moreover, of her five granduncles, two were also deaf .... In fact, the whole clan had to scream and shout, shout and scream.

Did they shout because they couldn't hear? Or had they shouted themselves deaf?

Two years. But the clamour and commotion she had left behind still raged on in the world. Her pair of bamboo chopsticks, tied at the ends with a flaxen thread, hung dusty behind the door, and they swayed and clattered lazily whenever the door was pushed open. I still remember the day when I rushed into the kitchen and, in the usual loud voice, shouted to her for the last time, "Have you cut yourself?" But I only saw her back — humped like a hillock — strands of dry silvery hair curling behind soft earlobes, and a few ginger slices spread out like gold coins beside her chopper. Nothing alarming had happened.

That is to say, there was no severed finger on the floor. But just then I really believed I'd heard the sound of a finger being cut off. I'd been in the next room reading a hard-cover edition of a philosophical text.

She jumped when she saw me. "The water will soon be on the boil."

"Oh, I've come to see whether your hands are ...."

"H'm, I'm heating water for washing hands."

The deaf are adept at making their replies seem sensible. Calmly and shrewdly, she went on with the guesswork, trying to figure out what I was saying and come up with an appropriate answer, determined to make people feel that there was logic to the world. I didn't correct her, I was used to her ways; I simply went back to my room as if nothing was the matter.

The sound rose timidly again. But it was no longer a simple slicing sound .... I pricked up my ears and seemed to hear the sound of things snapping and hissing and squeaking. That couldn't be the sound of ginger being sliced, it had to be the sound of a finger being chopped into pieces, of cartilage snapping, skin and flesh being torn off, and the knife catching in the joints. Yes, that was what it had to be. But why didn't she cry out in pain? All of a sudden, a round of almighty thumps exploded in the kitchen, so loud that the windows and doors trembled. I concluded that she must have got such a thrill slicing and cutting just now that she decided to do it on a grand scale. Was she slashing at her shoulders now? When she'd done her shoulders, would she hack at her legs? When she'd done her legs, would she go for her waist and then lop off her head? Bits of bone must be flying, blood streaming; and the blood, hot, thick and steaming, must be trickling down the table legs onto the floor, stealing its way into the corridor and, finding its way blocked by a plastic bucket full of chestnuts, turning, heading for my room ....

In desperation, I dashed into the kitchen again and saw — that nothing had happened. Her back bent almost double, she was slicing some dried bamboo shoots, bracts and all — she wasn't going to waste them.

Maybe something was wrong with me.

She caught sight of me and blinked, a bit flustered, "You want some hot water? I've just filled the flask. Lots of it. It's nice and hot, it just boiled."

I hadn't asked her any questions, certainly I hadn't mentioned anything about hot water. But perhaps to her, much of my silence — a large part of my existence — was not real. She thought that I'd said this or that and built up an illusion of me. I somehow got the same illusion too. But did she ever have the illusion that I had also engaged in such casual, mindless slaughter?

Once I had bought her a hearing aid. In those days, it was expensive and hard to get. Holding her tightly by the hand, I had dragged her onto one bus after another and crossed one busy street after another in search of the device. Being out turned her into a bundle of nerves, and she kept struggling to free her dry scraggy hand from mine — she couldn't help it, I knew. If she didn't have a seat on the bus, she'd be so scared when the bus started to move that she'd squat down on the floor and scream out my infant name, making me cringe with embarrassment. As she screamed, she'd stretch out her arms and grope desperately for the legs of the seats or for something else to hold on to. Sometimes her groping fingers would close on a pair of neatly-ironed trouser legs, and she would of course be cursed and glowered at. When we crossed the street, she never followed my lead. A look at the traffic would throw her into a panic, and she'd pull me back or charge forward, with enough force to make me stumble. If my attention wavered in the slightest, she would suddenly break into a trot, leaping like a youngster right into the path of a car that had come out of nowhere, as if she was playing chicken with it. Her self-confidence and stubbornness — typical of the deaf — always sent drivers into a blue funk. An apprehensive thought once crossed my mind: one day she'd lose her life under the wheels of a car — at that street corner perhaps, or perhaps in front of this litter bin. Poor Aunt Yao.

I got her the hearing aid. But ever afterwards she'd frown and grumble, "Maota, the thing's useless. I'm old, how much time can I have left? Why waste the money? It's no use." "How could it be no use? I've tried it, it works quite well," I said. Then I examined the device. As always, it had either not been switched on, or its volume had been turned to zero. "Don't turn it to high, it eats up the petrol (battery)". She watched reluctantly as I showed her how it worked, ready to turn down the volume again as soon as my back was turned; ready to wait till the next time when she could, with absolute conviction, grumble to me again, "Maota, the thing's useless, I told you so. I'm old, why waste money like that? Send it back, a petrol (battery) costs money, it's worth a lot of bean curd!"

To her, the world was perfect as long as there was bean curd in the house. Our whole family was brought up on bean curd; bean curd made us grow tall and strong, as tall as the door and solid as tree trunks.

And so the hearing aid was never used again. It was tucked away in a cloth bag she'd made, and the bag lay buried in the brazier box[2] which she used for storing clothes and which we never cared to examine. The earpiece, coated with a ring of dirt, looked as though it was still radiating warmth from a deaf person's ear.

And so we carried on yelling and shouting.

I had no idea how she lost her hearing, she had never talked about it. When I asked my father, he only said that she was ill when she was young, had a fever and ... But what sort of an illness? Oh, just an illness, couldn't remember now.

Everything the older generation in my family said was vague. They seemed to think that that was enough for the edification of the young and was a clear demonstration of their sense of social responsibility. They seemed to think, too, that that was enough to make us do what they saw fit — like eating carrots and taking aspirin

---

[2]A large wooden box containing a charcoal brazier, used in south China for warming hands or drying clothes.

and what not. So it was not until much later, when I met an old
woman on a boat during my first visit back to my home village, that
I heard a few stories which seemed to have something to do with
Aunt Yao.

An ancient river ran through a stretch of fertile mountain land.
Ancient pebbles of every colour lay scattered in its bluish-green
waters. It was said that in earlier times, the river was flanked by thick
woodlands and that bandits often raided merchant boats carrying
rice and salt up and down the river. Later on — no one knows when
— the local authorities sent people to fell the trees along the river
banks, and a road began to steal its way into these parts, allowing
the passage of carts and horses. Still later — again, no one knows
when — the authorities sent people to build a wall, like the Great
Wall in the north, in a bid to keep out bandits. Now, of course, this
little great wall was in ruins, bits of its foundations still barely visible.
A few rusty-looking stone slabs covered with withered lichen lay
crouching maliciously on the ground, hidden almost completely by
tall thorny grass. Several mounds of earth, no longer supporting
bricks, their edges rounded by rain and wind, sat there looking
like toothless gums. What had they eaten to make their teeth fall
out?

The old, sallow-faced woman was as thin as a blade of grass —
a single breath could knock her down. And she was so tiny that a
back-pack basket could easily accommodate three of her. Her eyes
and mouth were misshapen and looked like careless slashes made
in a piece of shrivelled cassava with a knife. Tears thick as glue filled
the two slashes above, which were brilliant red at the rims. She
looked half hawk and half human, and her features bore a slight
resemblance to Aunt Yao. She and the others on the boat spoke the
local dialect. For a moment, this made me feel strongly that my
home village was real; fate, too, was real, and I had a mystical
connection with this stretch of alien land. Now I was back, and in
my veins ran the blood that flowed from here — from this moun-

tain, this river, this village. And tests would have shown that it was the same blood flowing in all the passengers around me, including this old woman.

A tall strong young man, his face full of drinker's spots, was standing beside the old woman. Her son probably. It was hard to believe that she could have given birth to a living thing two or three times her size.

"Uncle Yao? Oh yes, I know her." The two crimson slashes on the old woman's face looked me up and down. "She was a fine and quick-witted lass back then. The year when the Mos lost their second son, they said she was a witch and insisted that your father should enforce clan discipline by burning her to death. The poor girl!"

"You must be mistaken. My aunt isn't ...."

"Oh? Isn't she Sister Yao from Yunjiadong?"

"That's right."

"Isn't her name Shuxu?"

"Yes, it is."

"I know her, too, I do. I know all of them, all the girls within thirty miles of here. No wonder you look a bit like her. She and I were born in the same year, she's a few months younger. Isn't Bearded Li her husband? That bastard used to go whoring and gambling, and he took ...", she rounded her lips as she lifted her hand towards her mouth and made a ring with her thumb and little finger, apparently to indicate that the man took opium. "His brother came back earlier this year. Said he'd come from afar to find his old house. I saw him in the street."

I stared at the crimson slashes and noticed that the pupils were not what you would call pupils. Was it infection of the tear gland, or conjunctivitis, or too much exposure to sun and smoke, or perhaps too much radiation from her memories, that had scorched them and made them fester?

"She was really down on her luck! When she gave birth to your eldest cousin, she was in labour for hours. There was no doctor then. So they asked Mangui to cut open her belly with a kitchen knife — just like they do when they slaughter a pig. Even then, the baby died. She wailed and howled, and then went deaf."

"I see."

"Is she still in Changsha?"

"Yes."

"In the city or the countryside?"

"The city."

"So she's enjoying life now. But I heard that she doesn't have any children. Pity!"

"She wants to come back."

"What's the point? Her house is gone. Besides, she doesn't have any children. No, she can't come back." She let out a soft sigh.

I had heard that people in this area attach great importance to having children. Women who can't conceive often spend nights sleeping naked up in the mountains to expose themselves to the south wind, since they believe that the south wind can make a woman fertile. Or they will drink a potion made from stewed bee hives and flies — a kind of folk prescription. They probably think that insects that reproduce in large numbers can make a barren woman fertile. If these measures do not work, the disgraced woman will take her own life or exile herself from the village, never to return. That was probably why Aunt Yao left her home and went to work in the quarry and serve as a nurse-maid. When she left the village, she had probably also taken this same boat. She had probably also seen the pebbles shimmering in the depths of the water — eggs laid by this skinny river after centuries of struggle.

The boat had rocked its way into a cool, shaded spot. It lurched, and a clatter of footsteps rose from the boat and went ashore. A group of girls carrying bamboo baskets on their backs suddenly leaned and pushed against one another and burst into loud giggles, no one knew what they were giggling about.

2

Lao Hei, too, had no children. Would she kill herself or live in self-imposed exile for the rest of her life? Of course not. There was nothing wrong with her whatsoever, she had declared to all and sundry, and she could have as many kids as she liked — broods of them. To prove the point to her mother-in-law, she rather indifferently got herself pregnant last year, and then had a minor operation in hospital to "get rid of it", as if she was doing it for kicks.

Sure enough, she'd done lots of things for kicks. She'd taken part in the revolution and sported an old military uniform, got married and got divorced, she went disco dancing and played with cassette recorders, cosmetics and the like, and fags and booze gave her a jolly good time. Everything she had on was imported, no domestic products for her. Her bra gave her support up top, a pair of jeans girded up her bottom, giving more than a little boost to her centre of gravity, and as she strutted forward on her long slim legs, she seemed to be gliding along on a cloud, ready to take off and soar into the sky. A woman like this could of course say, with a proud lifting of her chin and a graceful wave of her slim fingers, "I've got rid of it."

Of course she had to get rid of that mess of blood and flesh. How else could she disco forty-nine hours straight and then sleep right through three whole days and nights? How else could she keep indulging her whim of asking whoever she could get hold of to go for a walk with her in the dead of night, a cigarette dangling from her lips? How else could she go visiting on her motor bike and get the better of her men friends on whatever topics they were arguing about? How else could she still play her favourite game of tearing paper into shreds (bank notes would do when there was no paper, and when she had no bank notes, she'd borrow or snatch some from her friends), and then, standing on a tall building or a clifftop, watch as the confetti fluttered through the air before disappearing, and getting so excited she brayed like a donkey?

I found it strange that Aunt Yao should have such a god-daughter. I also felt that the reason Aunt Yao went to take a bath in the end had a lot to do with that sweet smile Lao Hei beamed at that chap Gong. That day, Aunt Yao had prepared a dish of fried fish, which she insisted on taking to Lao Hei, for she said Lao Hei loved it. But Lao Hei had long gone off this dish, I told her again and again. Each time she nodded her head, but whenever she cooked that dish, she would follow her own logic and convince herself yet again that the girl loved it.

I had no idea when Aunt Yao went out or when she came back that day. But she was in quite a state and started quizzing me at once. Did I know that big feller Gong? What kind of a person was he? Did he have any family?

I knew there'd been some kind of misunderstanding. Even if Lao Hei were to marry again a hundred times over, she wouldn't have settled for Gong. She had told me that Gong had admired her from afar and come to seek her out. She made him cry, made him kneel before her, and, having made a fool of him, told him to get lost. "The men in this world are as good as dead. They're all such sods!" Yet she couldn't bear not to have men around her, and so she greeted their flattery and their jealous rivalry with part disgust and part appreciation. Anyway, she would have found life intolerable if there were no men jostling for her attention.

I tried to reassure Aunt Yao at the top of my voice; she said "Oh," and seemed to believe me. But from then on she always looked somewhat depressed when she was pottering about the house, and she couldn't suppress her suspicion and resentment of that man. She kept muttering to herself, "Just look at him and you know he's no good ...."

"That man is not thirty-six. I'd say he must be well over fifty if he's a day ...."

"That man, I'm sure he doesn't have a proper job ...."

That man, that man.

Having reeled off yet again her usual unfounded accusations of that man, she went to take a bath. I should have foreseen that accidents occur most easily in the bath. Both Li, an artisan who lived in the East Wing, and Feng, the woman in Block Four, had a stroke, or suffered gas poisoning, while taking a bath. Maybe it was because human beings come naked into this world and wish to go naked from it. With its gaping mouth, the bath tub tempts people to take off their clothes, its evil designs all too obvious.

Aunt Yao had taken a bath only the day before, but she said she felt itchy all over, and bustled off to boil some water. Perhaps she was also busy with something else, I don't know. Anyway, I hadn't noticed and I didn't care. Heaven knows how she found so much to busy herself with. Apart from cooking, mending clothes, and grumbling about this one or that, she loved to hoard all sorts of junk. Bottles, for example. She wouldn't throw away even an ink bottle, let alone wine bottles, oil bottles, pickle bottles and glass jars. Tucked away under and behind her bed, they formed a dusty forest of bottles, a tribe of bottles a century old. She was fond of paper, too. Whenever I crumpled up a piece of paper and threw it into the dustbin, she would pick it out as soon as my back was turned, smooth it out, and stealthily add it to her collection of newspapers, wrapping paper, used envelopes that had been opened up ... etc., and then fold them into a square parcel which she stuck under her pillow. When the lump under the pillow grew too big, she shoved her new acquisitions elsewhere, often at the foot of her bed, and so there were little mounds here and there under the quilt which she used for a mattress. They made her mattress, and her life, a lot more substantial. When she really had nothing else to do, she would busy herself checking the time : when she saw the numbers flashing in one corner of the TV screen, she would immediately look at her old alarm clock. On seeing that the difference was only five to ten minutes, she would heave a sigh of relief, pick up the alarm clock, wind it, and then put it back into a glass box held together by adhesive tape. If the clock was keeping good time, she would exclaim happily:

"Maota, see how accurate it is. Look!"

"Yes, pretty accurate."

Even I was influenced by her, converted, to be precise; for I, too, acquired such a habit. Every so often, when I heard the time signal on the radio, I would instinctively call out to her, "Ten o'clock now. Is your clock keeping good time?"

"Yes, it is."

And I would feel relieved.

It seemed that she hadn't yet checked the time today. I should have sensed that something was amiss but I was having a good time with my friends. As usual, we exchanged a few jokes, puffing at our cigarettes, then we would talk about a certain distinguished economist for the hundredth or the thousandth time, or gossip about the latest rumours for the thousandth or the hundredth time, or sneer at the despicable conduct of some friend of ours for the hundredth-and-one or thousandth-and-one time — as if such a way of passing time was right and proper, was in keeping with the book shelves and oil paintings behind us; as if it was different in some significant way from Aunt Yao'ss diligence in checking the time.

My friends left, leaving a pile of cigarette butts behind, and I got rready for bed. I was about to get into bed when I felt that there was something I still had to do. Then I realized that the place was too quiet — usually I could hear a light snoring from Aunt Yao as she slept.

"Aunt Yao!"

She was nowhere to be found. Only when I tried to force open the bathroom door did I see, through the crack, clouds of steam filling the entire bathroom. They leapt at me like wild, ferocious beasts.

I saw a hand through the steam. She'd had it!

The doctor said she'd had a stroke and advised us to send her to the hospital, which was just pouring money down the drain. Both western doctors and traditional Chinese doctors shook their heads at her kind of paralysis and only promised to "have a go at it". I might even have to study the posters on the lamp posts in the street to seek out a travelling herbal specialist of some sort, or check the time-table at the railway station to take her to a big city for treatment. In that case, I'd need more money. I searched through Aunt Yao's pillow cases and her brazier box and found by chance a couple of mouldy batteries tucked away since god knows when, and half a jar of unused face cream discarded by some woman. Apart from these, I found only parcels and parcels of paper, bundles of frayed cotton wadding and some old clothes, including the scarves and cotton padded shoes we had bought her. They all smelt of mildew and exuded the stale musty odour peculiar to old women. I seemed to have searched through her entire mysterious life before I found a gold ear-ring that was worth a bit of money. I remembered the occasion when the accountant in her factory glanced at me knowingly and said, "Yes, she's been with us a long time, and she's indeed been a model worker once, we'll give her some help. But ..., how could she not have some money put by after all these years?" At the time, I was overcome with guilt, for the accountant's knowing eyes made me feel as though I really had enormous wealth hidden away. What a fool I'd been! Why didn't I have a good row with that woman in the black felt hat? But then I didn't know how to. If it had been Lao Hei, everything would have been fine. When she accompanied Aunt Yao to the factory that time to apply for a reimbursement of her medical expenses, she argued furiously with the people there about whether two bottles of blood pressure tablets could be included. Her verbal punches sent everyone sprawling and when she got home, she switched on the TV at once to watch a *kung fu* film.

Aunt Yao had once confided in me that her workmates had borrowed money from her — it might have been a few *yuan* or tens of *yuan* or even close to a hundred *yuan*, and they never paid her back. I said she ought to have a word with them, at least remind them about it. She looked terrified, as if she'd been told her head would be chopped off. Then she uttered a long drawn-out "well", her chin drawing back, her lips quivering, and mumbled, "No, I can't, I can't."

Then she laughed, "It's too embarrassing! I must learn to be Jiao Yulu."[3]

That was a long long time ago. Father and the rest of us in the family had encouraged her to learn from Jiao Yulu. I had even read her stories about him from the paper, being at the age when I was keen to show that I could read aloud from the newspaper. In those days, I was proud that I had an aunt who was a worker. I had no idea then that her factory was so dark, or that it was situated in an alley which was slippery and damp all the year round. It looked as if an old mansion had been taken over for the factory premises. The front door, dark and imposing, with shining brass knockers, opened with a screech and swallowed me whole. Bags of goods piled high straddled the corridor, looking as if they would come crashing down on me any minute. There was only enough space for the men and women working in the dark to squeeze past sideways. The dilapidated shed that was called the canteen huddled in one corner at the back of the courtyard. The cement floor had cracked, a few slabs had gone missing, and the dark soil underneath looked awkward and out of place. The windows had been nailed together from rusty metal scraps of various geometric patterns. The

---

[3] Party secretary of Lankao county, Henan. He led a life of extreme self-denial and devoted himself to promoting the welfare of the people. In the 60s, the Communist Party often urged people to learn from his example.

chopping board reeked of fish and two bowls of some dark substance sat on it. Drawing nearer, I heard a loud buzz, and a swarm
of black specks, which turned out to be flies, dispersed into the air,
revealing two bowls of rice. On the surface of the rice there was a
round depression marking out the bottom of another bowl, as if it
had been stamped there. As soon as I saw the flies, I had an
inexplicable feeling that Aunt Yao's deafness could never be cured.

Some women had gathered round to study a bowl of something.
One took it up and sniffed at it, another pressed forward to have a
look. Then they walked away, grimacing and shaking their heads.
They were all belching and rubbing their noses in satisfaction, as if
they had been prompted to do so by a distant droning from
nowhere.

"Has it gone offf?"

"It stinks. Yuck!"

"Where shall I go to perm my hair?"

"Take it further away before you throw it out. Don't spoil my
appetite."

"Pity. It cost fifteen cents."

"Go and fetch Deaf Qin, quick."

"Sell it to her for three cents. She'll take it."

"I bet it'll rain tomorrow."

"Old Wang treats her pretty well, it seems."

"Ha! Ha! Go on! You old devil!"

Someone was slapping hard at her thighs, and the far-off
droning turned into a loud blaring.

They didn't know me and went on gossiping freely about
Aunt Yao to add a bit of spice and pleasure to the food they
were gulping down. I saw a black gaping mouth with a glistening
copper tooth. Bits of the copper had worn away, revealing the
white lead inside. It was a sight I could never forget — it hit me
like a bullet and shot through all my sense of shame and amazement.

Perhaps these people had always belched and rubbed their noses in satisfaction — when they borrowed money from Aunt Yao, when they sent her to sweep the floor, or when they saw an irate patient calling her to clean the bed pan but she didn't hear. Later on when I told Lao Hei all this, she cried. I couldn't believe she could still shed tears so pure and clear. She even hissed: "Damn! I wish I had a machine gun — I'd mow them down!" I tried to make allowances for them but she called me a hypocrite.

I flared into an almighty temper in Aunt Yao's dormitory — a crummy place with uneven floorboards. She asked me to sit on her bed but I plonked myself down on the one opposite. She pressed some biscuits into my hand; I crushed them into bits and flung them onto the floor, saying they were no good. She had saved up lots of wooden bobbins for me; I could play with them as toy cars or stand them on end and pretend they were toy soldiers and bandits fighting a fierce battle. But I shoved them away, sending them rolling underneath the beds or into the corners of the room, scattering them like corpses on a battlefield. Even though I saw that she had been so taken aback she looked white in the face, her hands trembling, I still felt aggrieved and was still shaking with rage. I even wanted to snatch up that arrogant little round mirror by her bed and smash it to pieces!

I didn't know why I was behaving like this.

At a loss what to do, Aunt Yao forced a smile and then went to wash the dishes, her back bent almost double. But she did not forget to scrape the bits of left-overs carefully into a small brown jar, screw on the bakelite cover, and then place the jar piously on top of the black brazier box she used as a bedside cupboard.

She always used this jar as a food container and when she came to visit us after work, she would bring us food in it. When there was a feast of some sort in her factory, we would get bits of pork and fish.

Especially in the days after my father's death.

3

Father went away in the end. This man with whom I was so inextricably linked, on my curriculum vitae at least, always talked in whispers. When his colleagues dropped by, when Aunt Yao came, when friends knocked on the door, or when someone from his village visited him, he would send us out to play, and then close the front door and start to whisper in earnest. I stared sullenly at the door, my eyes travelling from the latch we used now to the catch installed by a previous owner, and finally to the few rusty screws which was all that remained of the latch put on by yet another owner, and I wondered how many owners the house had had and who they were. Ever since then, I had always felt that closed doors were very mysterious, that they had incarcerated my elders and made them old and weak.

Later on I came gradually to learn about some of the things my father had talked about in whispers. He had forced Aunt Yao to divorce that man and taught her how an oppressed woman ought to fight against oppression and to make a clean break with her past. Many years later, when Aunt Yao's hair had turned grey and the skin on her neck had grown loose and flabby, Father again discovered, in all seriousness, that there was some kind of demarcation between Aunt Yao and us. He warned Mother not to let us mention Aunt Yao again when we had to write essays on topics like "A person I know well". He also warned her not to let us go and play at Aunt Yao's place so often. One New Year's eve, when Aunt Yao arrived happily at our place for the family reunion dinner with a large basket of Spring Festival goodies, Father, after a whispered conversation with Mother, made her take Aunt Yao back to her dormitory in the factory. That day, I pricked up my ears and heard my father use strange expressions like "relatives of bad elements" and so on. I also heard him say to my mother, "... you don't understand ... it's the Spring Festival ... the work unit ... what would people say?"

But to us he said, "Aunt Yao is on duty today. When you go out tomorrow, you can drop by her place for a visit." Then he went out, chatted about the weather with someone he ran into, and tried to laugh heartily.

That was a terrifying New Year. Ever since then, I couldn't shake the feeling that whenever the grown-ups put their heads together and talked in whispers, something bad was bound to happen. And so I was dead scared of having to go for a pee in the middle of the night. For everytime I woke up, I'd hear Father and Mother whispering in their bed on the other side of the room, although before I went to bed, they always seemed deeply preoccupied with their own things, a solemn look on their faces. This gave me nightmares.

But Father still went away in the end. I used to think that his life was regular as parallel syntax, and steady and solid as a big dictionary. I used to think, too, that every Saturday evening he would stroke my head as I snuggled up to his big tummy, and would leisurely sing to me ('recite' was the word he used, though I'd say he 'sang' it aloud) a long poem, "The Road to Shu is Hard", or "Song of Everlasting Sorrow". And yet, he went away in the end — for a haircut. That was what Mother told me — he'd gone for a haircut. Now that I thought about it, I regretted that I hadn't realized that big-character posters had appeared in his work unit that summer. I regretted, too, that I'd gone with my schoolmates to a mountain village to fight the drought. I should perhaps have seriously asked myself why recently Father so often stroked me and patted me on the back to put me to sleep, and why he poked at the rat hole when he came back from work. There had been a time when there were rats all over our house. They would poke their heads out at the side of the door or from underneath the cupboard, squeaking noisily, or make a racket marching and scampering on the ceiling beams, or nibble with relish bits of cotton, dried bean curd, nineteenth-century history books, Cao Xueqin's work and grammar and rhetoric, or chew them into powder for lining the holes. But we had trapped and killed those rats long ago and restored peace in our house. Why did Father still poke at the long-deserted hole? Why did he, every so often, sigh and say, "Anytime now." Why?

At the time, however, I didn't think much about these things. And when I got back from the countryside, full of excitement, my things in a string bag on my back, I found Aunt Yao and Mother clutching each other and crying. The moment they saw me, they turned away, tears glistening in their eyes, and demanded, "Didn't your dad come to see you?"

"To see me?"

"Didn't he come to the village?"

Of course not, I said.

"Then where did he go? Where?"

Mother started to cry, and so did Aunt Yao. After some time, I heard vaguely the voices of other people trying to guess why Father had disappeared — Mayhap he'd gone to visit that Li somebody, or Wan, or ... I sensed at once that something terrible must have taken place these few days, and the house had become very very empty.

"When did he go?"

"Four days ago, four days! He said he was going for a haircut, but he hasn't been back. He took forty cents from me!"

We looked for him in vain for about a week. Every evening when I went to bed, I would hold tight to my mother's leg on my left and Aunt Yao's on my right to give them comfort and support. Their legs felt dry and cold, like the skin of winter bamboo. As I held on to this bamboo skin, stubble began to grow on my chin.

They finally found him. Two middle-aged men from Father's unit came from the local police station and showed us a photo. It was the blurred outline of a human head, every wrinkle on the face smoothed out, and the face itself bloated and shiny, like a fully pumped up ball. The expression it wore was one of impatience, as if it was about to sneeze but couldn't. Trembling with fear, I darted one glance at it and never looked at it again.

Was that him? I didn't know why, but I could never again remember his face clearly, maybe because my last look at him was too hasty, too full of fear, and too perfunctory. When my impression of him was at its faintest, I'd even wonder whether he had ever existed. But it didn't really matter. The person I called my grandfather — I'd never seen him at all. And what about my grandfather's father? My grandfather's father's father? ... Who were they? What had they got to do with me? The past whispers of this man or that one or the other, what had that got to do with my taking my kid to buy some bubble gum? With the fresh sunlight shining on me? With the pebbles I was about to tread on? Lao Hei never bothered with questions like these. And so she could stuff snacks of all sorts into her pocket. And so she could lift her chin proudly and say, "I've got rid of it."

Later on, Aunt Yao could come to our place as often as she liked. She always arrived at dusk, always came on the eve of a festival, and was always laden with her rush basket. That basket was for us a direct access to the market. It was a large mouth that poured out eggs, vegetables, fruit, clothing, new sports shoes, and things bought with her latest wage packet, and they soon turned into our sustenance, into an answer to our dreams. Out of that basket poured years of our lives. It was a magic basket, an inexhaustible supply of precious things. Even now, it hung there behind my kitchen door, dark and soiled, holding bits of charcoal.

As usual, Aunt Yao would draw an evening paper from her basket. She had always followed my father's decree of subscribing to a newspaper — even when the Party and Youth League organizations in her factory had quietly cancelled their subscription.

Sometimes, she would put down the paper, look at us over the tops of her spectacles, and lament with a heavy heart, "Maota, there's so much pain and suffering in Vietnam!"

Or she'd say, "Maota, philosophy is such a good thing. How come it's such a good thing? It helps you to understand things, all things!"

Or she'd say, "One mustn't be selfish, Jiao Yulu's own chair had fallen to pieces, yet .... If everyone was unselfish, the world would be a wonderful place, don't you think?"

Naturally I roared assent.

I didn't have much time for her. Friends dropped by; we puffed away at our cheap cigarettes, shook hands firmly in greeting or at parting, as if we were about to embark on some solemn death-defying mission, and once we got started on the October Revolution or the rural survey, the discussion would last the whole night. We lived as if we were in some film or novel, and this feeling made us wear our tattered jackets with more flair and flamboyance.

It was Lao Hei who was more attentive to Aunt Yao. Behaving like a true goddaughter, she'd snuggle up at Aunt Yao's feet, look up at her and tell her about Gorky's *Mother* in a voice loud enough for her to hear. She even told Aunt Yao that when the revolution was over, there would be luxuries like washing machines, televisions and robots, everyone would live in comfort and peace, and Aunt Yao would no longer have to do any chores.

Aunt Yao was overcome with amazement and disbelief. It was a good while before she mumbled slowly to herself, "Would life really be so good? It'd be worth dying for, wouldn't it?"

We all laughed, none finding any deep meaning in her words.

In her spare time, Aunt Yao would just stay at home. She didn't like to go out, not even to the park, or the cinema, or the theatre, or simply to drop in on her neighbours for a chat. Even in June, when it was baking hot in the house, she was reluctant to take a chair out and sit in the shade. She preferred to stay inside with the door closed so she could keep a watchful eye on the shabby furniture and the few pickle jars in the house, and to keep up the vigilance she had dutifully lived with all her life. As soon as the door was closed, her towel — a piece of blue cloth torn from a pair of old trousers and hemmed with coarse thread — was safe. Safe, too, was her teacup with its make-shift lid — a round of cardboard stitched at the rim — and the bloated tasteless tea leaves which she must have retrieved surreptitiously from a visitor's cup after his departure. Likewise, her umbrella was safe. Made of black cloth so heavily patched that the threads alone weighed at least two ounces, the umbrella could never be either opened or shut properly, and it nestled behind the door like a big bird poised for flight. As for the stainless steel telescopic umbrella I had bought her, it was, not surprisingly, nowhere to be seen.

She had been sitting there a long while, and for a long while she had not made a single sound. I glanced at her. She had dozed off, her hands tucked deep in her sleeves. Her head rolled slowly to one side, and then nodded with an abrupt dip. She jerked back her head, wiped her runny nose, ran her tongue around her teeth, moved her lips as if she was munching something, and swallowed. Then her head rolled slowly to one side again, dipped abruptly again ....

I nudged her gently and urged her to go to bed.

"Um, Um." She made some noise to show that she was awake. I had no idea whether she meant she would, or would not, go to bed; or whether she simply thought that some sort of a response was enough.

"Go — to — bed!"

"Um, the fire hasn't died out, has it?"

"Go — to — bed! Do you hear me?"

"Yes, yes. I'm reading the paper."

She picked up the paper again and forced herself to read a bit longer. In a while, I saw that the paper had slipped from her hands, and her head was again lolling and nodding. A string of snot hung from her nostril, about to fall.

I again urged her to go to bed, this time more obviously

impatient. She looked slightly embarrassed, pinched her nose and wiped her fingers on the heel of her cloth shoe. Then she grinned and said, "You don't understand, Maota, I can't sleep if I go to bed too early." At other times, she'd say, "It's still early, still early."

And yet she had obviously dozed off just now. But then she probably believed that going too early to that hard and narrow bed of hers was a luxury, an indulgence punishable by death, and therefore she had to say no to it politely a couple of times before she could set her mind at ease and allow herself a good night's sleep.

One day, she bought some eggs that had gone off. A smug expression on her face, she told me it was a good bargain and that she had saved these eggs especially for me. I didn't know whether to laugh or to cry and didn't touch them. This would have been all right; but I mucked things up by opening my mouth, and I didn't mince my words. The eggs were no good, they weren't fit for eating; they'll make you sick, throw them away. I knew that I'd fouled things up the minute I opened my mouth, but it was too late. At once, Aunt Yao did the predictable: she gauged the situation quickly and assumed what she considered to be her responsibility. Recovering immediately from her surprise, she picked up the bowl of stone cold rotten eggs, place it right before her, and said she could eat them. Yes, she could. I made things worse when, instead of coming to my senses, I foolishly allowed myself to show my concern for her by exclaiming involuntarily, "They'll make you sick!"

My words made her grow even more polite. She smiled, unperturbed, and said, "Yes, yes."

"What do you mean — yes, yes?"

"A lot of oil and salt have gone into this dish. What a waste to throw it away! Eating eggs make you sick? Nonsense!"

To prove her point, she picked up a large piece with her

chopsticks and stuck it into her soft, broad mouth. My hair stood on end.

Finally, I snatched the bowl from her and threw the rest into the toilet. She was furious, she pouted her thick lips and made a racket in the kitchen, thumping pots and pans and dishes and bowls. She finished all the chores, not forgetting to heat some water for me to wash my feet, but there was an icy expression on her face, and she grumbled sourly about me as she went about the house-work, "Never seen anyone like that, never! If I'm such a pain, why not take a knife and finish me off? I don't want to live anymore, what's there to live for? What? What? Why waste food on me .... I'd like to crawl into a hole in the ground. At least I'd get a bit of peace, but I just can't find one. I don't need to be told I'm a pain, I know it. I'm worse off than a grasshopper. But these old bones won't die, I can't help it! What can I do ...."

For days on end, she was like that. She even tried to make up for my wasteful deed by finishing off all the leftovers, including the scraps that dropped onto the floor. She stuffed herself till she came down with a fever, went weak in the limbs, couldn't even open her eyes, and looked like a straw that had withered in the sun. Naturally this led to a series of fierce confrontations between us — shouldn't she take some medicine? Shouldn't she drink boiled water? Shouldn't she slip a pillow behind her back when she sat up in bed? Should it be a pillow or a pair of cotton padded trousers? .... It amazed me no end that she should be so clear in her mind when it came to judging what was good or bad for her, and that she should opt so instinctively for that which would harm her. To get her own way, this frail woman relied on her adamantine politeness and self-control, and victory was always on her side. Needless to say, a fierce battle of politeness broke out between us, sweeping to one side the original cause of our dispute and blowing the whole thing out of proportion.

Meanwhile, my stubble grew into a beard.

4

I saw a hand through the steam. Then I saw a dangling arm, which was in fact just two sticks of bone wrapped loosely in old skin. But the skin was not coarse. Rather, its scaly, powdery surface reminded you of a snake that had just sloughed its skin. Then I saw the head with its sunken temples and hollow eyes. These depressions, and the gaping hole that was the mouth, made the head looked uncannily like the skull it would eventually become. The hair, wet, matted and soapy, was plastered over one side of the head, exposing the white scalp at the roots, and gave you the feeling that the mystery of women lay entirely in their long hair, for their scalp looked quite ordinary, even coarse and ugly, certainly not so very different from that of some bald fellow. Then, I saw a flat shrivelled chest with collarbone and ribs sticking out so sharply they would probably break through the skin in time. The nipples, two blobs of darkness stuck carelessly on the cage of bone, grown long and thin, probably out of a yearning to give suck, now drooped forlorn in despair. Falling away below the ribs were deep creases made by the rope belt used to hold up her trousers, and then the jagged twin mountain peaks that were the pelvis, the whole enclosing a space big enough to accommodate a great world. The belly was heavy and sagging, weighing down the skin so that its wrinkled curves and loops looked like a heap of mud slithering slowly down a wall. Of course, I also saw the shiny scar midway between the waist and the belly, and one side of her skinny buttocks at an oblique angle. I saw, too, in the parting between her thighs, sparse pubic hair floating in the water. The surprising thing was, her legs were full and rounded, their outline soft and smooth, and they were translucent, like white marble — the legs of a young woman, really, and still good enough to rock-n-roll beneath a mini-skirt.

It suddenly struck me that one of her hands was missing. I collected myself and looked more carefully. The hand was still there. I tried hard to wave away the steam.

It was the first time I had seen Aunt Yao's body, the first time I had ever seen the real her. And this white silhouette seemed so foreign, so awful, I dared not go touch it. It was as if this woman, who had never been a mother, still retained the chastity of a virgin which I must not profane. At that moment, I could not help but wonder what Aunt Yao looked like when she was young. I had seen a photo of her then. Faded and yellow with age, the photo showed a few enchanting women wearing lipstick and cheongsams. It was hard to tell which one was her, hard to know what sort of a mysterious world was linked to the lipstick and the cheongsam.

Lao Hei, too, had beautiful legs. How would she look when she was old? Would she, smelling faintly of foreign perfume, her body wrapped in imported clothes, turn gradually into a shrivelled date?

Lao Hei had once remarked, "Aunt Yao," (then she said in English), " — must die!" She lifted her chin and looked seriously at me, then she flicked a cigarette out of a packet and said, "It's cruel to let her hang on like this. It's perfectly humane of us to let her die. We can easily set up a suicide scene, no problem at all." At this, every cell in my body exploded, my heart nearly collapsed, and my eyes bulged till they hurt. Then I heard the hospital lunch bell.

A sneer flitted over Lao Hei's face, and her slim body went strutting out of the hospital and never came back again. I knew that in the past few days she had sweated and toiled looking after Aunt Yao — bathed her, fed her, helped her with the bedpan; and her kindness extended even to the stranger in the next bed. All this was real. But she would never come to the hospital again, and this, too, was real. The generosity she showed when she was touched and the viciousness that surfaced when she was ruthless — both were real. She was a person who lived a real life and was completely honest to her feelings. But how dare she lift her chin like that when she talked to me, with such nonchalance in her voice, about the possibility of

murder, real murder! The watch she used to have was a gift from
Aunt Yao — the sweaters, too. And her travelling expenses to and
from the country were also provided by Aunt Yao. And now she
wanted to .... No doubt, she would find this logic of gratitude vulgar
and ridiculous. She would certainly cite some deep and profound
philosophy to show how flawless her arguments were, just as she
would, when topics like *qigong*, music, or sex came up in conversation, say with a condescending sneer, "You don't understand." But
we were not dealing with a theoretical question now. No! To dress
it up as a theoretical question would make it less real. She had no
right to draw at her cigarette with so much panache, as if she were
a knight errant or a gifted scholar.

She hadn't always been like that. Aunt Yao, too, often said this
to me. I remembered the occasion when, having gone to the city
for medical treatment, Lao Hei was preparing to return to the
countryside, back to the rural unit where urban school leavers were
despatched for labour. To test her revolutionary zeal, she decided
to embark on a "long march" by braving the snow and returning to
the countryside on foot — a ten-day journey. We were stunned when
we received her telegram, and went three times to meet her. We
were lucky the third time. Having staggered along for over five miles
deep into the heart of a mountain white with snow, we finally saw a
dark spot wavering at the end of the road and recognized her
grubby padded jacket.

But now she simply didn't want to talk about such trivia from
her past. No point. What she was most keen to talk about was, of
course, people — men as well as women. She swaggered into the
room, confident, self-assured, and, caring not a fig who was there,
she would take the floor at once and go straight to topics which
excited her interest. On a certain woman — her eyes, the bridge of
her nose, her body, hands and feet, the way she dressed and the way
she carried herself — Lao Hei could make such fine observations
and come up with such unique views that the men would at once

accept her as one of their own. Then, looking as if she was a little
uneasy, she would scratch her head and say, a touch of self-mockery
in her voice, "Isn't it strange that I should think just like you do? It
makes me almost a man!" And she would move on at once to talk
about men, at a level where even the men would not venture.
Pleased with her performance, she would then throw a few teasing
remarks at such men round her as were clumsy in speech, or red
with embarrassment, "Too much for you, hey? What's wrong with
your nerves? OK, let's talk about something else." And talk she did,
until everyone had left. It was a good thing that Aunt Yao was deaf.
If she were able to hear what spewed out of Lao Hei's mouth, she'd
certainly have had a stroke long before that fateful day in the
bathroom.

But then Lao Hei didn't care what Aunt Yao liked or disliked.
Just as she didn't care about the views of the factory supervisor or
the manager. If she wanted a day off, she took the day off. She didn't
bother to inform her boss. And she didn't pay a blind bit of
attention to the notices in the park. She just behaved as it pleased
her — plucked a flower or two, picked some fruit, a look of
innocence and delight on her face. An outing without such adventures would bore her stiff. She was on familiar terms with all sorts
of people in the city — writers, painters, movie directors, singers
and dancers, quite a few government officials and their children
and relatives, and even foreigners, black or white, working in the
consulates. Connections. Yes she had connections. That was why
she was in the position to turn her nose up at Aunt Yao and at all
and sundry, even though she was always going on about how filthy
society was, so that she had to head straight for the bath as soon as
she got home, and soak herself until her hair, done up in cudgel-like
clips and rollers, was thoroughly drenched.

True to her word, she never came to the hospital again. I went
to look for her, to ask her whether she had ever heard Aunt Yao
mention someone called Zhenxu. For lately Aunt Yao was always

mentioning the name. There were many messages left on Lao Hei's door — from Zhang, from Ma, from M .... A bearded man with a large leather suitcase who had stationed himself outside the door scowled at me, as if I had no right to stand there frowning and rubbing my hands. When I found her later on, she had already changed jobs and was some sort of a temporary worker in a shop that sold painting materials. The telephone line was poor, and her voice sounded distant, as if it was coming from the moon, "... Zhenxu? I guess she must be Huang Ai, the one who distributed food coupons. Is Aunt Yao still alive?"

"Yes." My reply wasn't as forthright as it should have been.

"If you're short of money, get it from my place. It's in the drawer. The key to the front door is in the same old place." Then she hung up. I knew for a fact that she was generous with money, most of the time, at least.

But money was not what I needed. What did I need then? Time, of course. I needed time, needed every hour, every minute, every second to do my reading, to argue with friends, to run around, to do what I had to do — things which I'd regret as soon as they were done and which I'd also regret if they hadn't been done — and to express my bewilderment and amazement at this city. But Aunt Yao had returned from the hospital and had started to pound on her bedside table again.

I went at once to look for the bedpan and the diapers. They had been washed and were still warm, having been hung beside the fire to dry.

"No. I'm hungry. *Hungry.*"

She was demanding lunch again. I looked at my watch, it was not quite eleven yet.

"What do you want for lunch?" I asked her, trying to retain my cool and not to think about the blobs of spittle gathered at the corners of her mouth.

"Meat!"

She thumped mindlessly on the table again, and the thunderous bang and its vibrations made my mind reel, all the parts inside it cracked and dislocated.

She had a good appetite lately. Three large bowls of rice per meal, and lumps of meat. Pork with lots of fat especially — she would gobble it up like it was bean curd. I was surprised, for she hadn't eaten pork in the past. She had told me that in those years in the village, the heads of those who had been executed were often chopped off and hung up as a warning to the public, and when the ropes wore through, the dark lumps would fall to the ground and the pigs roaming the village would gnaw at them, sending them rolling, often into the gutter just below her window. She said that since then, the mere sight of pork made her feel sick.

And now, she had grown fond of pork. When a freshly-prepared dish of pork was taken to her, she would sit up at once and gorge herself so heartily that even when the grease trickled from the corners of her mouth onto the front of her jacket, she wouldn't notice. Yet she kept complaining that we were stingy and didn't provide her with meat to eat, repeating over and over that she was old and couldn't eat much. What made things more difficult for us was that when she was in the hospital, she bitterly accused the domestic helper for having eaten, behind her back, the pork we sent her so that she didn't get a single piece of it, though even the patient in the next bed said good-humouredly that she had eaten it all herself. Our helper pulled a long face, and said she had never come across such an impossible old wretch. We assured her that Aunt Yao didn't used to be like that, but she refused to believe us.

Aunt Yao seemed to have changed. The person who had emerged from those clouds of steam was someone who only looked like Aunt Yao. Even the expression in her eyes was different, for it often revealed a viciousness alien to me. I shuddered as I thought about her. Finally, I realized that this was a malicious plot on the part of the Creator, whose aim was to make her arouse the hatred of every one around her and to destroy all our sympathy for her and all our fond memories of her before letting her die. I felt that this plot followed me everywhere I went; I couldn't disentangle myself from it, I could only act in compliance with it, one step after another, and yet I'd no idea where it would take me. A crow was cawing outside my window, an old man selling ice often popped his head in through the door — what was the significance? I just couldn't figure out what mysterious messages of enlightenment they carried.

It would perhaps really have been better if Aunt Yao had died in the billowing steam. I shivered at the thought, and wanted to go at once to sweep the floor or wash the vegetables. As a matter of fact, Lao Hei had said something similar a month and three days ago. One month and three days. Was that the difference between me and Lao Hei? Was that what my aspirations amounted to? If it was, wasn't the world a little too fragile?

Aunt Yao burped and said with a frown that the meat was tasteless. It'd be nice if she could have some fried fish. I had fully expected her to say this, and so I pretended not to hear.

"Some more rice?"

"I want fried fish."

"Some cabbage?"

"I want fried fish, fried fish an inch long."

My wife couldn't stand it any longer. She leaned forward and spoke into her ear, "They don't sell fried fish any more."

"They do? That's good, that's good."

"No — they — don't."

"They don't? Nonsense. Go to Taiping Street, I used to get them there. Go and look. Taiping Street."

"That was — ages — ago!"

"Look around for a bit. Maota, don't be stingy. Your Aunt Yao is old and can't eat much. Don't be stingy. You should help me, should learn from the example of Jiao Yulu, you know." She seemed to have read my mind, and smiled mysteriously, waiting to see how thoroughly ashamed of ourselves we would become.

Then she reclined in bed, closed her eyes, and nodded off. A little while later, she began to snore lightly, her lips quivering like the fluttering wings of a bee, while the red speckles on her face looked as if they would burst through the skin.

I did go and buy some fried fish. I rode so hard on my bicycle a screw at the pedals fell off, and I knocked down a man on the street and had a row with him. But I knew that fried fish still wouldn't make her happy. I was right. First, she said there were no fermented soya beans in the fish; when my wife brought her some, she said there was no garlic; when my wife brought her some garlic, she said there was no salt; when my wife brought her some salt, she still wasn't pleased. After a few perfunctory jabs at the fish with her chopsticks, she frowned as usual, put down the chopsticks, and sat there glumly. I asked her what was the matter, but she only mumbled to herself: it was nothing like the fried fish she used to have, it couldn't have been bought at Taiping Street, no wonder it was so dry and bland. Oh well!

In the old days, she did go to Taiping Street very often. To get some fermented bean curd — my favourite snack — she would brave the rain with her rickety umbrella and be gone half the day. Sometimes she would even go on foot just to save some money. Her good impression of Taiping Street had been engraved on her mind and would never fade.

Her suspicion of things like the fried fish turned into resentment against us, into hostile vigilance towards my wife in particular. When my wife went to help her relieve herself, she would pull a long face and turn down her help. As soon as my wife's back was turned, she would shit freely in bed. And so the drying rack at home would have an extra load hung on it, and my wife woould have an extra mess to clear up. The situation would be slightly better if I went to help her. She would look less stern and less hostile, sometimes she would even give me a smile. And sometimes she would whine, a little too like a weak and fragile child, when I gave her the elaborate massage treatment that helped speed up her bowel movement. My wife asked me, when we were alone, whether it was because Aunt Yao had lived a widow's life at too early an age that there remained in her the desire to behave like a clinging and defenceless child before a man.

There was no knowing, of course.

When I was not at home, or when I was at home but too busy to pay her any attention, she would tap irritably at the table. As time went on, she got into the habit of tapping at the table, probably because she found it handy to do so, and because she was pleased that she was still aware of certain sounds in the world. And so she tapped more and more frequently, tapped harder and harder, as if in supplication, or making a declaration of faith. The table top was painted black, but now a patch of paint had worn off, revealing the original pale colour of the wood. With its cracked grain, the table top looked like the skin of a drum with beard-like lines radiating from the centre, forming a pattern like that of a luminous star. Gradually, a depression appeared where the centre of the drum and the luminous body was, and it looked as if in no time the table top would turn into a plain simple basin. I was amazed: how could that scrawny hand of hers, with its coarse skin and knuckles like bamboo nodes, have the strength to knock out a depression on a wooden surface and not get hurt? Rap, rap, rap, rap. I felt that the sound was growing louder and more vicious; it smelt of blood and its reverberations filled the entire universe.

She rapped till our flat began to draw people's attention. At first, people peered in, or tapped at our windows, or shouted my name over and over to protest against the din. When they knew that there was no stopping it and that they simply had to live with it, they accepted the situation grudgingly. After all, they could still carry on with their own business — they could eat their meals, water their plants, make charcoal briquettes, repair their bicycles, chat about wages and the cost of living, put up a tarpaulin shed for a funeral rite, or play cards and mahjong. A few elders would, as they played their card game, move their table to where the building would provide shade, and so, in the course of a day, they would have moved their table from west to east, making almost a complete circle round the building, just so to stay out of the sun. One day, one of the regulars at the table did not turn up, and was never seen again. I had the feeling that the centrifugal force of their revolving movement had flung him out, and into the tarpaulin shed over on the other side.

Someone from the local housing department came to examine this old rickety brick building. He said it was in danger of collapsing, and recommended repair work in his report. I felt somewhat guilty, for I believed that the loud tapping from our flat had brought damage to the entire building.

A young couple below us was always screaming at each other, allegedly because the wife couldn't get pregnant. I felt guilty about that too, believing that the loud rapping from our flat had a chilling effect on their constitution and their relationship.

I began to go bald. Every morning when I woke up, I found strands of hair on the pillow, enough to roll up into a little knot. I also got into the habit of jabbing at rat holes. I would search through the flat and then jab at the holes with a bamboo pole or a pair of fire-tongs, and tell my wife to roll up her sleeves and give me a hand so we could do it in a big way.

I also quarrelled with people more and more. One day, Guojun dropped in for a chat, his hair neatly combed. As usual, he complained about the lousy management system in his work unit, and talked about democracy and bureaucracy. I had wanted to agree with him, there was no doubt about it. And he must have known where I stood, which was why he could talk so frankly and eloquently, and make so much noise cracking melon seeds. And yet, when I opened my mouth ..., I couldn't believe my ears. To hell with democracy, I said, it was damn ridiculous. On seeing how flabbergasted Guojun was, I went on to elaborate my point with gloating self-satisfaction: what was democracy? The suppression of genius by the mob! Truth was perceived only by the minority, it always was at the beginning, wasn't it? And wouldn't you agree that benevolent dictatorship was a thousand times better than democracy, which was really just a show? .... As I pontificated, I also cast him a stern look, as if I had long perceived that he couldn't make it to graduate school, and would never get that 18-inch colour TV he had wanted so much to buy.

Guojun's face went white, and he beat a hasty retreat, even forgetting his umbrella. My wife, looking a little annoyed, scowled at me as she cleared the table and the ash-trays, and complained that I shouldn't have got myself into such a state. Fake cigarettes were everywhere these days. Damn! They smelt terrible, worse than mosquito repellent — I said gruffly, also feeling a bit surprised at the way I had bellowed at Guojun just now.

Rap! — Aunt Yao started to rap on the table again, and was whining for attention like a spoilt child. I went at once to pull out the bedpan and to snatch a nice, warm dry diaper from the drying rack.

When the flurry of activity was finally over and there was peace again, my wife leaned her head on my shoulder and asked me gently, "Tired?"

"Go and check the stove."

"It's hard, but there's nothing we can do."

"You go to bed first."

She let out a soft sigh and said, "Grandpa Ming next door said that this is Aunt Yao's way of collecting the debts we owe her."

"Collecting debts?"

"Grandpa Ming said that all the favours she's done to the young will have to be fully repaid. He said that Aunt Yao has got 'creditor's paralysis'."

"Do we have any more cigarettes in the house?"

"Grandpa Ming also said that Aunt Yao wouldn't go until after she'd collected all the debts."

I thought about it for a while and said, "I see." Then I picked up the summary of a seminar on industrial planning for a tri-city economic region again, but I had lost my place. The summary boomed and rumbled in my mind.

5

I shouldn't hate Aunt Yao, if only because of that rush basket behind the door. It wasn't fair to her. But I could do nothing about it. When the clouds of steam wiped clean the other Aunt Yao that had been hidden away and repressed for years and pushed it before me, it was too late and I could do nothing about it.

The woman that was still called Aunt Yao — I can only describe her in this way — kept accusing our domestic helper of having gobbled up her pork on the sly to starve her to death. This, and the smell of urine that stank up the house, made all our domestic helpers, young and old alike, pack their bags in disgust in less than a week. It was hard to get domestic help those days. The women who were crowded cheek by jowl outside the agency were always whispering to each other, keen to find out which private enterprise company had jobs to offer and what the overtime pay was. The minute I walked into the din, I felt I was a beggar or that I'd shamelessly snatched money from these women's pockets.

I went early one morning to knock on Lao Hei's door, hoping to work out something with her, and was greeted by that long, narrow and prominent nose of hers. Blinking in amazement, she asked, "Is it getting dark already?" and from inside the house came the blast and boom of heavy metal percussion.

The noise and her unconventional greeting reduced me to silence. I stared blankly at the Japanese commander's sword and the mouldy helmet hung on the wall and it was a while before I said, "I've borrowed the material you wanted on folksongs. Are you getting ready to write poetry again?"

She tossed the remains of a cold bun onto the table. "What's so great about Glasses Qiao? I'll fight him to the bitter end, I swear!"

I repeated, "I've borrowed the material you wanted on folksongs."

She said, "It's strange, I keep hearing a light rapping from under my bed lately."

"Some sort of repair work downstairs?"

"No, I've gone upstairs and downstairs to check."

I glanced at the space underneath her bed. There was nothing except a few picture frames and a pair of dirty stockings. Nothing strange should happen there.

And so I went home.

And so I had to work something out by myself. Finally I learnt from a distant relative that Zhenxu and Aunt Yao had become sworn sisters a few decades ago, and that Zhenxu was still living in our home village now. I suggested to my wife that we could send Aunt Yao to Aunt Zhenxu's place. Of course, this arrangement ..., well, there was nothing wrong with this arrangement. To return to their home village — isn't that what all old people want? Wouldn't the fresh air and the water in the country help her recover more quickly? Weren't the houses in our village more spacious and wouldn't there be more people to look after her? ... We could think of a dozen reasons to convince ourselves and to prove to ourselves how pure and selfless our motives were so that we could, with an easy heart, discuss industrial planning or peel an apple or what not.

I finished peeling an apple and gave it to the neighbour kids walking past my front door. I didn't know why their parents looked so surprised — was it because they were taken aback by my generosity?

Of course, I had never seen Aunt Zhenxu in my life. In fact, I'd never seen anyone from my home village. And so I imagined that it was very far away, farther even than the moon. I even wondered whether the sun there looked too real to be true and whether it was the same sun that shines on us all.

My relatives sent me a reply, sent Aunt Zhenxu's sons along as well. They dragged Aunt Yao away from the house, put her in a bamboo deck chair mounted on two shoulder poles, and carried her away. I was surprised that Aunt Yao should have been so reluctant to go and that she should have made such a show of her emotions, calling me heartless and all that. But it was a good thing she did, for my heart, heavy with grief at the parting, hardened with real apathy all of a sudden.

Time passed. I learned that she was doing quite well in the village.

Time passed. We talked less and less about her.

I was grateful to Aunt Zhen. I had no idea when she and Aunt Yao became sworn sisters, or why, or whether the story of their relationship was dull or gripping. Just as I'd no idea why my folks told me that our ancestor was a spider, why there was the word "xu" in the names of most women in my home village, or why the people there addressed their wives, daughters, sisters, aunts, and sisters-in-law alike as "xu" and didn't use the conventional terms of address which indicate their positions in the family hierarchy. Some scholars said that the practice of communal marriage in primitive times had left its mark in the language and that this was one of the surviving linguistic traces of such a practice. I was taken aback when I learnt about it, but of course it had nothing much to do with me. It was only because of Aunt Yao that I learnt there was an Aunt Zhen living in a large dark timber house, with two protruding wings and an entrance hall hidden well away from view, forming a doorway that seemed dark and scheming. It was said that such a doorway could swallow monsters. A luminous mirror was hung above the door. I was told the mirror stood for the sea, for our ancestors' birthplace, and could keep away all evil spirits. As you went through the doorway, you stepped into a world of darkness and it was a while before you made out the lifeless shrine looming before you, with an altar full of offerings to the ancestors and other unknown gods and spirits. Like other timber houses in the area, this one also stood at a slant, and looked from a distance like a large black dog sitting on its haunches. These timber buildings were different from the brick houses, which stood upright and erect, and were set out in neat order, full of dignity and nobility. I felt it was because the bricks and stones had died, while the wooden beams and planks still had life in them even after they were felled, and were still struggling to live on, growing in all directions, distorting the houses into weird shapes. These buildings often stood together, each with its own distinct style, each guarding its own secret.

Beautiful flowers were often seen in front of these timber houses. The bright reds of peonies and dahlias blasted the peace and quiet of the green surroundings. But the mountain people didn't pay them much attention.

Going downstream on the narrow river, one saw groups of timber houses here and there along the bank, forming small villages, looking like flies resting on the mountain side, motionless. The current was strong, and the boat glided swiftly down the river. Then the water began to lash at the boat with increasing strength, and there was water and spray everywhere, like a pot on the boil. Needless to say, the boat was "shooting the rapids". The boat-owner was tense. The boatmen at the helm and at the bow held tight, blue veins standing out on their limbs, and they picked their way in the water with vigilant eyes, shouting to each other in jargon the passengers found hard to understand. The river was like a precipitous slope, and the boat seemed to be diving headlong down a steep slide of water. When it dipped at the bow, huge sheets of water splashed into the cabin and drenched the passengers. But the boat-owner shouted loud warnings not to stir, not even to make a noise. All of a sudden, the boat slid towards a whirlpool the size of a pond, and everyone was seized with panic. At the last moment, the boat swerved away, no one knew how hard the boatmen had fought against the current just now, or whether it had all been an optical illusion. The boat seemed to be moving at breakneck speed, and yet looking up, the green shore didn't seem to be shooting past any more swiftly than when the boat was moving in calm waters. Perhaps the boat hadn't moved at all in this land of foam and spray. But then, all of a sudden, you felt that the raging water had receded, and when you turned round to look, the boat was already at a safe distance from the rapids. In a flash, it had covered a few miles, leaving well behind the lone lighthouse overgrown with moss.

On approaching the even more dangerous rapids, the boat-owner would, for safety's sake, ask the passengers to get off and do a stretch on foot, so that he could shoot the rapids with an empty boat. As one walked along the weather-beaten earth embankment, one could hear the clinking and hammering of the stone-masons working on a bridge. No doubt a wide road would soon penetrate into these mountains. One could also hear the dull thud of people felling trees and making rafts. The mountain people were about to send the rafts, made of cypress and *nan*-wood, down the river. Once there, the rafts were hauled ashore and sold as timber, and there would be no mix-ups about which raft belonged to whom because of the different markings on the timber. Sometimes, one would even hear the hoarse blaring of *suona*[4] from afar and then run into

---

[4] A Chinese wood-wind instrument.

a group of young men performing some ritual, each holding in his hands a wooden basin lined with red paper, on top of which was some maize, or grain, or a row of paper notes neatly laid out. No one knew what those things stood for, or what sort of ritual it was.

The boat was now steering its way through a deep pool. The water was clear, and smooth as a mirror. Ahead, the mountains on both sides moved slowly apart, tearing open a slit of sky that grew wider and wider. Behind, the mountains were quietly moving together, forming a screen that closed off the sky. They call it the Mountain Gates. When the boat arrived, the Gates opened; when the boat had passed through, the Gates closed. There was one mountain gate after another, beckoning, inviting you to venture further and further into the beyond, towards a green islet or a stony beach, towards a place where *someone* seemed to have stood waiting for a long long time.

Along the river bank were dark grey cliffs, with boulders large and small, piles and piles of them heaped upon one another, each with sharp edges and corners, wide crevices and deep holes. The boulders looked arid and desiccated, and reminded one of charcoal — maybe the shrubs and bushes that had forced their way out through the crevices were tongues of fire blue and green, a fire lit by the gods in heaven which, burning since ancient times, had scorched the peaks so that they cracked and broke into all those lumps of charcoal that strewed the river bank.

Here, "city" is a vague and remote concept. Breathing the air, so fresh, so green, you wonder why people would want to leave the mountains and the river for the city, to be pushed and jostled by the crowd. Is the city anything more than a pile of faeces dropped from the golden arse of the sun which then hardened? Is it anything more than that?

Once on board the boat, you were in the boat-owwner's home, and he played host to all the passengers, offering them cigarettes and tea. If anyone felt like it, he could crawl into the cabin, slip

under a worn-out quilt and take a nap. The boat-owner told us about
the handsome income made by his mates who dredged sand, about
his adventures when young, and he pointed at the hilltop to our
right to show us the boundary wall. He said that it was about eight
feet high and its foundations five feet deep. His grandfather had
been recruited to build the wall and in those days the pay was good
— for every three yards, you were paid twelve cents in silver. He also
said that in those days there were many barracks and sentry posts
and the guards had to go on patrol day and night, rain or shine.
One year when the bandits were on the rampage again, each of the
guards on patrol would tuck a cured human heart in his bosom to
fortify his nerves.

The boat rocked unsteadily as the passengers leaned over to get
a better view of the little great wall. Then they shouted excitedly —
Yes, I see it. I, too, strained my neck and eyes, but I didn't see it.
How strange! I saw only a lush gentle slope and yellow butterflies
fluttering over rippling grass. Not only was there no boundary wall,
it didn't even seem likely that any momentous events had ever taken
place there.

They saw it. What did they see? Could it be that their eyes were
different from mine?

I went ashore and up a flight of stairs to the jetty. A little further
on, there were a few sheds selling food, a notice about taxation, and
a set of two pedlar's boxes with a carrying pole, the boxes displaying
a silversmith's glittering goods. The local people were bustling
about; some were gathered in twos and threes whispering into one
another's ears, as if they were trying to keep something from me. I
kept feeling that someone was calling me from behind. I turned
round and saw a dark-faced man calling his daughter.

I went into a small shop to buy a packet of cigarettes. There
were a few thin, sunburnt old men sitting round a small table. The
way they talked bore such a close resemblance to my father's speech
that I was stunned. Some of them were smoking a bamboo pipe,

some holding a small wine cup. They darted a look at me, as if they already knew who I was, and then they went on talking in hushed tones. From their expressions, I guessed they must be going over that story about the guards who went on patrol with a cured human heart tucked into their bosom.

The shop owner smiled at me and remarked that I was an honoured guest. Then he asked me where I was from, what brought me here, and whether I needed a place to spend the night. If I did, he said, it'd be cheaper and more convenient to stay here in his place rather than in an inn. I had just started to introduce myself when I saw a flash of recognition in his eyes and heard him utter an "Oh". He had already guessed whose son I was, and he also told me my father's name as if he knew him quite well — it seemed that the village folk could talk about each of those who had left the village as if they were their own family members. The other old men sitting idly around also nodded and grinned at me, baring their stained teeth. There was one amongst them who probably didn't know my father well, and the others, in their languid way, began to explain to him who my father was.

Across a dry ditch from the shop, there was a large playground with a tumbledown basketball hoop and a two-storeyed brick building. On its walls, the faint outlines of slogans painted in lime, slogans like "In Education, Learn from the Dazhai Spirit", could still be seen. The children were having a good time, screaming and shouting, dashing here and there, kicking up hot yellow dust that soon settled into a thick layer at the foundations of the walls and the foot of the pillars. The shop owner told me that the building right in front of me had in fact been the site of my ancestral home. In its day, it was a grand mansion. There were three courtyards separating three groups of buildings, spacious balconies, elaborately painted and carved beams and pillars, and a large back garden. The whole mansion was protected by a high fireproof wall a little distance from it. An impressive place indeed, he said. They only pulled it down when the school was built. In those days, when the tenant farmers delivered grain, they would cross the river and then enter the granary through the back door. They had trodden smooth the footpath that ran alongside the embankment. I could indeed see that smooth footpath — cool, light, delicate. The side near the ditch was covered with a film of moss. It looked strangely familiar. This footpath, I thought, had drawn boatloads of grain from the river and provided sustenance to my family, and to me, who was still living and breathing. Ah! So that was it. Father had always refused to let me visit my ancestral home because he was afraid I would see this footpath. He must have known that the moment I set eyes on it, it would rouse me to rebellious disobedience.

The shop owner told me all this casually. And, breaking off every now and then to provide some light-hearted rejoinder to his customers who were discussing something to do with beef, he also told me where my fifth uncle had been shot — by some peasants who had risen in rebellion.

I knew for a fact that that dandy who excelled in horse-riding and gun play was shot to death. There were a few other people executed along with him. My grandfather was so terrified when the shot was fired that he lost his hearing. The deafness was handed down to Aunt Yao. Of course, the history of deafness in our family could perhaps be traced to an even earlier generation, to the generation before that, and the generation before that .... What had happened in those days?

"Did you know my father well?" I asked him abruptly.

The shop owner smiled, "Sure. I'm not bluffing. When he left here to go to school in the city, he went by boat, my boat. I also provided him with food all the way. At that time, your family had gone downhill, your folks had to survive on gruel, and your Aunt Yao had been dragged away at the end of a rope by Bearded Li. But the gods were kind to your father. One day when he was jabbing at a rat hole at the foot of a wall, he discovered two bundles of silver dollars inside ...."

"Jabbing at a rat hole?"

"That's right. He went wild with joy, snatched up the money and ran. His two elder brothers didn't know what the matter was, they ran after him but couldn't catch up with him. If it hadn't been for those two bundles of silver dollars, how could he get a chance to go to school? But come to think of it, it's really because your ancestral tomb stood on such a propitious site. I was there when it was dug up to make way for a road. I saw it. It was full of snakes, each about a foot long. There were so many of them, enough to fill half a basket."

"Did he ever come back?"

"He did, though I didn't see him myself. I only heard about it from someone." He turned towards the others, "Qin's third son came back for a while, didn't he?"

A bald old man cleared his throat and muttered tonelessly, "He did. That year he came back to turn his father in to the Farmers' Association."

By now, my eyes had got used to the dark and I was able to see the elders more clearly. Their hair had been bleached to a dull brown by the sun, and it curled at the ends as if it had been slightly singed. They were dark all over, down to the crevices of their fingers, the backs of their ears and even the roots of their hair. They seemed to have just been scooped out of the huge oil cauldron which is life. Firm, compact, smooth, solid, resilient, a nice weight in the hand. They were studying me; their eyes, firmly fixed on my face, were busy prying, dredging, excavating, trying to dig up someone they knew. It was an unbearable intrusion, it dug so hard it all but forced open my skin, pierced and broke my skull, and it penetrated to the mass of grey matter in the deepest recesses of my brain. It occurred to me that only those used to watching people being decapitated or buried alive, to seeing human skin being torn off, living bodies being cut up inch by inch, or people shot down by firing squads —

only those people, and their descendants, could stare at you with such unbearably intrusive eyes.

In silence, I asked for blessings on them, on all the strangers here. I had come to visit my home village, to visit Aunt Yao. Poor Aunt Yao, she had died. I received the telegram two days ago. And it was real this time, not like last time, when Aunt Zhen's eldest daughter-in-law made a mistake and raised a false alarm. Maybe because of that absurd experience of bereavement I'd gone through, I felt calm this time, I didn't cry inconsolably. But then you couldn't anticipate whether you'd cry, for it seemed that grief came in a fixed quantity — once you'd suffered a measure of it, there would be a measure less. On receiving the telegram, I thought about practical things only. I had to take a few days' leave. Maybe the folks in the village would want to send her off with all the customary rites, in which case, paper money had to be burnt, a cock had to be slain by a fortune-teller, a banquet had to be arranged for the living, the grave had to be warmed before the coffin was lowered, and a ceremony had to be held to invoke the spirit of the dead. I needed money for all this. Of course, I also had to make her a traditional robe in the style handed down from our ancestors in order to observe the ancient custom — "Surrender when you are alive but not beyond the grave".[5] I knew nothing about the origin or meaning of this custom. For whom had our ancestors changed their costumes in submission? To whom had they surrendered? And how did that initial practice of burying the dead in the costumes of an earlier dynasty develop in secret into a widely observed custom and get handed down as an iron rule for perpetuity?

---

[5] Allegedly this is the agreement General Wu Sangui made with the Manchus after the fall of the Ming dynasty. It meant that the Ming people would adopt Manchu customs when they were alive but not when they died. So they wore Manchu clothes and hair style during their life but would be buried in Ming costumes.

I left the shop and walked into a willow grove. The grass was dense, pointed blades swaying weakly, thousands and thousands of them. The sun was so strong the bronze swords were half-broken, close to melting. It was quiet on this lane. It seemed as if *someone* had just departed.

I saw again the hazy mountains in the distance. I saw here and there the remains of the boundary wall that had once crossed the hills and climbed the mountains; it looked like a broken line struggling to heal, to become one again. And I saw the sun, a tiny white spot, like the eye of a cooked fish.

6

Aunt Yao had a keen and delicate sense of taste. She wanted to eat hare, and so Aunt Zhen's eldest son cycled to town at the crack of dawn, a distance of over five miles of bumpy road, to see if he could come upon a couple of hunters with dead hares dangling from their blunderbuss. Then she wanted to eat ricefield eels, and Aunt Zhen's second son rolled up his sleeves and his trouser legs, and waded slosh slosh in mud with a small bucket, occasionally calling down curses on himself by trampling others' rice seedlings. But since no one in the family except Aunt Yao ate those things, they were roasted or cured or salted and carefully stored for her consumption. But she couldn't eat much. She would just pick at them with her chopsticks, and then pull a long face, turn away from the food, and start to grumble. What had displeased her? Was she bored? The two brothers had a word between themselves, and one went to look for a bamboo bed, the other to braid some ropes. Then they tied a knot at each end of the bamboo bed to make a stretcher of sorts, and carried their aunt out into the open to cheer her up. They carried her to the threshing floor and the river, and to see the ducks, the butterflies and the long-haired rabbits raised by a particular household in the village.

Every day after work, the brothers gave her this treat. The bamboo bed creaked as the ropes cut into their shoulders again and again. They trotted from place to place; their vests, soaked in sweat, flapped noisily in the wind, and they wiped away beads of perspiration dripping from their chin.

"Hoo — ray, hoo — ray —" Aunt Yao was pleased at last.

She was particularly fond of peddlers and the loads they carried on their shoulder poles. As soon as she saw a peddler, she would insist on a closer look. Her face lit by the myriad reflections of the wares as the sun shone on them, her eyes narrowing into slits, she would smile happily at the coloured paper windmill for kids, and purse her thin lips, hooraying with joy. "Buy one, Damao. Don't be stingy, I've got money. Buy one!"

So they bought her one.

She had money, no question about it. Apart from the monthly pension she received from town and the money sent to Aunt Zhen for looking after her, she had one hundred *yuan* tucked away at the bottom of her brazier box. She remembered it clearly. So she fished out the money and asked Aunt Zhen's eldest son to get her one windmill after another, sticking them in front of the window so they could turn freely in the wind. Once, Aunt Zhen needed some money to buy a manure bucket and some piglets, and helped herself to a small loan from Aunt Yao's box. Aunt Yao was peeved when she learnt about it. For days she complained that someone had nicked her money, and kept muttering that she had to write to Maota and ask him not to send her any more money. To get her own back, she pissed and shitted in bed, and thumped the edge of her bed methodically, making the planks bounce up and down, so noisily that the animals in the pigsties started to whine and scuttle about hysterically, thinking, no doubt, that the end of the world had come.

Aunt Zhen, on her part, felt she had been wronged. Her face bloated with anger, she screamed at Aunt Yao, "Thump, thump!

Thump yourself! Who nicked your money? I've only borrowed it. I'll pay you back today! Today! Now!" She shoved a few grubby bank notes into Aunt Yao's box and went on, "I never owed you anything in my last life, and I don't owe you nothing now! Why do you give me such a hard time? Sister Juhua gave me a hard time, Fourth Sister gave me a hard time! I've never had a single day of quiet, not since I came here as a child bride at the age of five. And I have to live with this dreadful toothache. The wretched basin has started to leak, there's no mending it right. And my husband is a beast! You're the only sister I've got left, what good does it do you to torment me so? What do you get if I die?"

The outburst over, she slumped on the floor and burst into tears. Aunt Yao, too, cried, as if she was still capable of understanding something.

She could understand what had been said, she probably could.

Aunt Zhen had often said that it was she who kept watch at her sisters' deathbed, and she was sure that Aunt Yao would die in her house, too. She made these remarks when she was at her neighbour's place. She loved visiting her neighbours. Never known for being a discreet person, she would say anything that came into her head and wash her family's dirty linen in public — her husband, that ungrateful sod, slept around with sluts; her second son still wet the bed not so long ago, shame on him! She would curse and swear when she touched on something that riled her, and burst into boisterous laughter when she was pleased. But now she couldn't drop in on her neighbours as often as she liked. Nearly every day she had to wash a bucket of clothes stained with urine or soiled by faeces. Nearly every day she had to stay at home to help Aunt Yao turn over in bed, or wash her and sprinkle talcum powder on her back so that she wouldn't get bed-sores. Aunt Zhen felt that the men shouldn't be asked to do these things, so she did them all herself. She sweated and toiled till her eyes were bleary, her toothache got worse, and she would swear at her husband as she nursed her aching cheek with her hand. The brothers couldn't bear to see her like that and wanted to send Aunt Yao back to the city. But their mother said enigmatically — How could you? Remember the soft-shelled eggs we got from the hens the last few years? They were an omen. She'd long known that Sister Yao would come one day to give her a hard time. But they were sisters, and that was that. It was the will of heaven! She had to put up with it.

The brothers failed to make her change her mind, so they carried out their plan on the quiet. One day, they struck a deal with the owner of a sand-dredger and were about to send Aunt Yao away. Their mother learnt about it. Her face changed colour, and she tucked half a bottle of pesticide into her bosom and said darkly, "You're right. It's time we went. Anyway, I don't want to live anymore. You want to send us away? Then send us all the way to hell." Her second son nearly had a fit. He tore at his hair and stormed out of the house, and for over six months he stayed with his friends and didn't come home.

Aunt Zhen's eldest son, who was better at coming up with ideas, tried to work out how he could make life easier for his mother. In the end, he found a way. He cut out a hole in the middle of Aunt Yao's plank-bed, another in the middle of her bedding. On top of the hole, he put a movable lid, below it, a bedpan. Aunt Yao had only to remove the lid and stick her bottom into the hole to relieve herself. No hassle.

And yet Aunt Yao seemed to hate that hole. When the time came, she would sneak a look around and then shit and piss straight onto the bedding to show that the plot would not work.

Aunt Zhen's eldest son was deep in thought again: why not convert the plank-bed into a lattice-bed? It'd be good for ventilation, and Aunt Yao wouldn't get sores all over her body. Besides, it'd be a neat and tidy set-up, she could relieve herself just as she liked, and her excrement would drop through the crossed laths onto the sand and ashes below. Ashes and all could be swept out from below the bed every few days and dumped into the pond. As for the quilt she used as a mattress, that would have to go, of course. A pair of thick open-crotch pants would do just as well. Besides, the cicadas had started to chirp, she wouldn't catch cold.

It would seem, perhaps, that she was being kept like a pig and not being treated with respect. But, well, if one gave the idea a bit more thought, one'd realize that it was respectful and necessary.

Further improvements were devised, still with respect. For example, her head was shaved to prevent lice from growing in her hair, a wooden trough replaced the porcelain bowl lest she should break the bowl and cut herself. As for shutting her up in a cage specially made for her, that was of course done later on out of even greater consideration for her. Anyway, the innovative measures really worked. Aunt Yao's sores gradually turned into scabs; soon, the scabs fell off, leaving pink patches of tender flesh. But very few people now would fetch and carry for her, certainly not as they had done in the past, and she felt bored and neglected. She couldn't spend the whole day taking naps, snoring and spluttering through parted lips; she had to find something to do, something to look forward to, something to plan about. The paper windmills were no fun now, and she had lost interest in Aunt Zhen's reminiscences about the past and the opera stories she told her. "Maota!" She called, staring at the beams on the ceiling, "Maota! Come here, come!"

She mistook someone sent to the village by the local authorities for her nephew in town. The young man, who had come to inspect the pigs, walked past her room. On catching sight of him, she insisted he was Maota. And she pinned the blame on Aunt Zhen — the woman had time for the opera, time to look at what they call "the bicycle", and to poke her nose into other people's business, like the row between the couple next door, but no time to go and look for Maota; even though he was here, she'd deliberately kept her in the dark.

She got very excited, and started to whine like a spoiled child.
But the looming silence soon turned her whining into frustrated
expostulation and angry denunciation until finally the voice, gasp-
ing for breath, was a mere whimper, "Oh, you heartless lot, go and
look for Maota. Why does he hide from me? Go and tell him, I need
medicine, I need medicine! He's got to find some for me. He's been
to school, he knows how to get things done. Tell him to go to
Shanghai, or to Beijing to get it. I need medicine! When you're ill,
you need medicine. Or there'll be trouble. I need medicine, go find
him, tell him not to be stingy ...."

Whinge, whinge. Until she nodded off again, her mouth still
open.

Aunt Zhen knew that in situations like this, she had to stay away
from Aunt Yao. Otherwise, she would get even more agitated, there
would be a dazed, intense look in her eyes, the veins on her temple
standing out like so many earthworms, while her limbs would grow
agile again with hatred, and her fingers would stretch and clutch
convulsively, like the tongue of a snake hissing with rage.

People in the village had started to talk: this nasty disease Uncle
Yao had — was that not heaven's punishment on her for bearing
no children? Or was it nemesis, for something bad she'd done in
her last life? They talked and talked, about karma and fate, until
they got the shivers, and wanted nothing so much as to go and take
a look at this woman who was doomed to die a terrible death. Then
someone else remarked that two cows in foal had lost their calves,
and insisted that the barren woman had brought bad luck to the
village and should be driven away or quietly burnt. But no one dared
to take any action, because Aunt Zhen was quite a strong woman,
and because the kids in the village were fond of her and extremely
loyal to her. In the end, people just whispered angrily to one
another when they walked past Aunt Zhen's house.

Aunt Zhen often sat outside her door mending clothes and
making shoes, or preparing swill. One moment, she would mutter

to herself, counting the faults of her sons and grandchildren. Another moment, she would chat and joke with the kids in the street. She wouldn't allow any stealthy glances to creep over the threshold, nor would she allow Aunt Yao to drag herself out of the house with the help of a small wooden stool. If she caught the slightest movement out of the corner of her eye, she would pick up the handy bamboo rod she had placed beside her, and make a quick swipe with it. Smack —! That shadow would invariably draw back to the other side of the black charcoal line drawn on the ground. For Aunt Zhen had ruled that no part of Aunt Yao's body could cross this line.

"Going out again? Again? You idiot! You want to get yourself killed?"

She then swiped at her own plump bare foot with the bamboo rod to punish herself for her rough treatment of her sister. They were quits now.

It took Aunt Yao some time to appreciate the authority of the bamboo rod. The first few times, she yelped with pain. Later on, she just groaned. Finally, she was tamed. When she saw the bamboo rod, she would behave herself and sit huddled up on the other side of the black line, lick her lips slowly and slowly turn her gaze to the small depression washed into the soil by the water dripping off the eaves.

"Go back! Go to bed at once!"

"Ooh! Ooh!"

"You've got your open-crotch trousers on. You look a sight! Shame on you!"

"Ooh! Ooh!"

"Your Maota hasn't come. He's busy. How could he spare the time for an idiot like you? He won't come, he won't."

"Ooh! Ooh! Ooh!"

Aunt Yao smiled fawningly, like a child who knew that she was in the wrong.

Aunt Zhen, too, came to realize how useful the bamboo rod was. When Aunt Yao refused to relieve herself, or to eat, she only had to pick up the bamboo rod and Aunt Yao would behave herself.

But then she couldn't sit there with the bamboo rod all the time. One day, she pondered on this for a while and then shouted to her eldest son, "Damao, come and do something for me. Make me a cage."

I had, later on, seen this bamboo rod. It had been left in a corner by the door. The handgrip had been stained by sweat into a patch of gleaming maroon and the other end worn down into a soft, smooth tongue-like shape the colour of the grey earth. I had seen the cage, too. Or perhaps I should call it the cage-bed. The part where the body had lain was smooth, the rest of the cage was made of thick sticks of China fir. The parts where the hand would not easily or often reach were thick with grime, making the cage look even heavier. Wooden wedges had been driven firmly into the mortise joints, and the wedges had been hammered so hard they were frayed at the thick ends — they made the cage look firm, solid, and unbreakable. When I finally set eyes on it, the cage was locking up a palpable mass of emptiness and loneliness, incarcerating a disappearance that could never really disappear. There were two entirely different worlds inside and outside the cage. Staying idly inside the cage, would one feel that it was the *outside* world that was under lock and key?

I was astounded that Aunt Yao could actually go on living inside that cage. Did she have such an amazing grip on life and such energy because she had never borne any children? Aunt Zhen's two children had told me how incredible she was: hunger and cold didn't bother her; in winter, she went without a padded jacket and crawled about on bare limbs, yet her palms were even warmer than the young men's. When Aunt Zhen opened the cage to help her put on more clothes, she snarled and scowled at her; she didn't want them.

There were other mind-boggling things which even the local doctors could not explain. Aunt Yao began to shrink, her wrists hung down and curled inward more and more, and her skin became drier and coarser until it finally cracked into patches of furrowed, delicately interwoven lines. Her nostrils began to flare and the narrow ridge between her nostrils and her upper lip grew longer and longer. One day, it suddenly occurred to people that she was a little like an ape.

She continued to shrink until her hands and legs were short and thin, as if they were about to crawl back into her body. If you just cast a cursory glance at her, you'd only see a bare smooth body, puffy eyelids, and a pair of dull expressionless eyes in which the white of the eye was dominant. And then one day, people hit upon another discovery: she was like a fish!

The fish flopped about inside the cage. It loved to eat uncooked vegetables, raw meat, grass and even the earth it could scoop up from around the cage-bed. When she had stuffed herself, she would giggle quietly to herself.

If she was not allowed to eat these things she would fly into a temper. Using that hand-like flesh-hammer of hers, she would thump her bed, making the planks jump up and down.

Bang! Bang —!

The grown-ups had almost forgotten that she existed. When a census, or an immunization programme, or any other such programme was carried out in the village, she would always be left out of it. When Aunt Zhen's neighbours gathered round the fire in her place in the evening, they wouldn't pay much attention to the rhythmic thumping or the intermittent burst of quiet giggling coming from that room. When they enthused over the new products that were all the rage in town or about the more well-known opera troupes, they would still burst into laughter that exploded in the air.

The kids, however, still remembered her. They had tried several times to sneak into Aunt Zhen's house, but Aunt Zhen flew at them and they took to their heels. But on market-days, or when the grown-ups had all gone to the fields, they would gather together again and egg each other on. Then, seething with excitement, they set off for that mysterious, forbidden place. They climbed on one another's shoulders till they reached the latticed window, and peeped into the dark room. Finally, they saw a pile of clothes inside the cage. They saw, too, that the pile of clothes could move. There was elation all round.

"What's that?"

"It's ..., it's a fish-man, isn't it?"

"Will it bite?"

"Salamanders bite, not the fish-man."

"The fish-man probably can sing."

"Dare to touch it?"

" 'Course! I'll even touch its nose."

"It's crying."

"Oh! I got a tummy ache."

"It wants to come out and play, don't you see?"

....

The kids felt that since this creature didn't have sharp teeth and a pointed tongue, and since it was kept at Aunt Zhen's house, it should of course be counted as a friend. So they tiptoed along the foot of the wall until they came to the back window. One of the window bars was missing, and they climbed in through the opening. Then they opened the cage door, the side door of the building, and, quite unnecessarily, all the doors in the house. They had created a free world — a world where one could come and go as one liked. Then, half hauling and half dragging it, they carried the creature out of the house. That done, they couldn't resist playing daddy and mummy to it. They fetched a bucket of water and gave the creature a bath, making sure that its bottom was scrubbed clean. Then they smoothed out the few silvery threads on the creature's head, plaited them into a single braid standing at the crown, and tied up the braid with a piece of red cloth. But they had probably made the braid too tight, the creature grimaced with pain and finally burst into tears. The kids were taken aback, and tried at once to cheer it up. One little girl said, "Stop crying. Look, the white tiger monster is here, it'll pounce on anyone who cries and take her away in a basket!" A slightly older boy came up with an even more brilliant idea. He tickled the creature under its armpits, the others followed suit. The children started to giggle; finally, the creature, too, had a fit of giggles. Encouraged by its response, the children all pressed forward to show their skill. Crowns of black hair squeezed together; everyone got into the swing of it, tickling the creature at its legs, its waist, its neck. The heads rose and fell, rose and fell ....

The creature laughed heartily. But after a while, murky tears filled its eyes. It was said that she had mumbled something, but no one heard what she'd said.

It was also said that someone did hear what she'd said — she'd mumbled something about a bowl of yam.

I had no idea whether Aunt Yao died that day. Anyway, this was all that I'd heard from my folks young and old. As to what happened since that day, no one had mentioned it at all. I had no idea how she died either. But whether she died of illness or starvation, of laughter or of sorrow, or whether she died because of the cold, the heat, or because her stomach was too full ... it didn't matter, and there was probably no need for us to think that death had to be related to these things just to make ourselves feel more secure.

I sat beside the fire in Aunt Zhen's house, a bowl of sweet tea — always served before dinner — in my hand, listening to the quiet dark night in the village and to a certain faint whistling sound that seemed both there and not there. The four small dishes on the table were filled with crispy sweet corn, pumpkin seeds, sweet potato chips and sweet rice pops. A delicious aroma filled the air, making it richer and heavier. When the dishes were almost empty, Aunt Zhen took them away and came back with large bowls of meat that had been pickled in earthen jars. In addition to pickled fish, pickled beef, pickled pork, and pickled venison, there were pickled chillies, pickled garlic bolts, pickled onions, pickled radishes, and pickled ferns. They made a feast for the eyes. There were also skewers of yellow slippery things. I thought at first they were pickled beans and only learnt from Aunt Zhen's eldest son that they were in fact pickled earthworms. But that was not all — underneath the pickled earthworms were pickled snails. I had long known that people in my home village love pickled food, but the feast today was a real eye-opener for me.

I took a look at Aunt Zhen. She held herself very straight, her hair was neatly combed, and one side of her face glowed in the firelight. She had large hands, large feet and large breasts, the front of her village-style garment was large, and her broad trouser-legs were also large. She talked and laughed in a loud, large voice. All in all, she had a relaxed and straightforward largeness that enveloped you at once and touched you to the quick, so that you wanted to snuggle up to her large plump bosom. She kept saying apologetically to me that the meal was "not respectful", and she asked me again and again whether the food was "bitter". I knew that by "bitter" she meant "salty" — people in my home village make no distinction between the two.

She picked up two lumps of pickled pork with her chopsticks and her eyes began to water. Your Uncle Yao was with us when the pig was brought home, she'd seen it grow, she'd even helped to prepare the swill. But fate was cruel to your Uncle Yao, she didn't live to eat the meat. Then Aunt Zhen put two lumps of pork into the bowl in front of the empty seat beside me and mumbled, "Sister Yao, try some."

The bowl was placed in front of an empty seat, at the edge of an immense dark night.

Sister Yao, was it bitter? Taste it.

The seat was still empty. Where was the person who should take the seat? Who was it?

She held up the corner of her sleeve to dab at her eyes and then helped me to more food. I heard a voice — dry, shrivelled, halting — squeezed out from her throat, "Your Uncle Yao missed you, she wanted you to come ...." I nodded, I felt that I understood what she'd said, and what, out of fear, she had refrained from saying. For when I walked into the empty house this afternoon, I suddenly heard, from out of nowhere, a loud sound of metal hitting upon something, like that of a steel sword upon the rock. A while later, she came out of the inner room whispering with a dark-faced man. The man said, "Xu, Wang of Heng Bay also knows." She replied gruffly, "So what?" The man asked, "Is it really thick?" She said, "Yes, it is." The man again asked, "You sure it's thick?" She said, "Yes." The man glanced at me, gave me a baffling smile, and quickly left. At that moment, I felt I'd understood everything, understood how Aunt Yao died — wasn't it because Aunt Zhen had caught sight of some cockroaches on Aunt Yao's face and had snatched up a knife and stabbed her to death? That loud clang, that whisper, that baffling smile, and that strip of plaster on Aunt Zhen's right hand — they were evidence, hard evidence. I also believed that at the time, Aunt Zhen must have been so panic-stricken that she shrieked and wailed so that all the kids in the village burst into tears. And that bald creature, contorting with pain, would have bared its teeth as if in a grin, while its left eye, still open, would be staring at a nearby bamboo basket. Then, in the tearful eyes of the children, the creature, so like a fish, started to swim ....

I had heard from the village folk that that year when the government tried to rout out the bandits, Aunt Zhen had gone up into the mountains and hacked two bandits to death with a sabre. Why could she not take the life of a fish then? Besides, it seemed to be a decree from heaven that she should be the one to bring an end to the long long life of this fish.

I gulped down the maize wine. My body started to burn and my head was heavy, as if it didn't belong to me. I looked at the sparks leaping from the fire, they went soaring up to the dark ceiling and then died out, one after another. They seemed far far away, at some remote corner of the universe.

7

I woke up too early. It was pitch-black. When I closed the door, Aunt Zhen was still fast asleep, deep in a dream of sweet harvest. There was really no need to go to the market at such an hour. The butcher and the old woman who sold fried buns would still be at home, but I kept feeling that I ought to set out a bit earlier, to walk along the moon-drenched mountain track, and to be the first to greet the sun. I groped in the dark, and half-stumbled into the market place. Then I banged my head against something, a tree probably, or one of the poles of a food stall. A throbbing pain at my temple, I opened my eyes wide and looked around me, finally I made out a narrow, dark and winding shore line running along a sea of scattered stars and realized that the shore line must be the street with its shops and houses.

I didn't know why, but I still didn't see any lights, nor did I hear the sound of cocks crowing and dogs barking, of people coughing and doors creaking opening. Could it be that it was only the middle of the night and my watch had deceived me? I shook my watch, took a deep breath, and pressed on. Suddenly, I stepped on something soft. I darted back and felt instinctively that it was something fleshy and slippery that had scurried off into hiding. It must have been a snake. I had taken a step back, but my other foot also hit something soft. It scrambled away from under my shoe, but it was probably too frightened, for it went scampering up my trousers and all the way to my waist, its paws scratching my skin. It was a good thing I slapped myself in panic, for it fell into the dark with a plop. I broke into a cold sweat, the shivers creeping up my spine, and my legs went so weak I dared not move at all. I held my breath and listened, there seemed to be some light rustling noise on the ground. I looked down, and saw many dark shadows flitting past me. Heavens, rats! So many rats! So many rats fleeing for their life! Why?

Suddenly I remembered. A group of people had arrived at the village a few days ago, and they had been going round the village lugging a tripod and other equipment with them. They had also called a meeting to find out whether anyone had noticed any unusual phenomena — cocks flying up the tree, for example, or a significant rise in the water level in the well. In addition, they had urged the villagers to adopt a uniform warning signal, to keep watch at night on a rota system, and had ordered all inhabitants of brick houses to move into timber houses .... And so the young men in the village who had been to school sstarted talking about something called earthquake. Could it be that what I'd seen just now was the first sign of an earthquake? Why else would the rats come out in full force? Had they sensed that a fierce battle was about to break out below the crust of the earth?

Was this earthquake caused by Aunt Yao's thumping fist?

Aunt Yao had died. The village folk said she had in fact come back to the village to deliver some money to Aunt Zhen, for the money she had received from town these few years was a lot more than what she actually needed. But Aunt Zhen didn't want any of her money, and used that sum to arrange a grand funeral service for her instead. But then Aunt Yao didn't need that either, did she? She was deaf all her life and not used to people fussing round her, what was the point of sending her off on her return journey with pomp and ceremony? She was lonely, childless and friendless all her life, what was the point of ending her last moments on earth with such fanfare?

That day, the firecrackers exploded noisily in the air, bursting into golden clusters before they died out, riddling the day with gaping wounds, blasting and charring it beyond recognition. Dark, melancholic notes rose and fell from the *suona* and drifted in the empty space before you, behind you, sawing gently at the shimmering light of the sun. Blowing at the *suona* were a few slovenly dressed hunchbacks and blind men, some with wooden expressions on their faces, others staring blankly at a rock before them, or at a blade of grass by the roadside. They paid no attention to one another, didn't even look at one another. At the sound of the drums and cymbals, they slowly licked their lips, ballooned their cheeks, and blew into their instruments. With what seemed a professional numbness, or a sorrow so well hidden it was completely unnoticeable, they followed the lead of the torches and the knives that were slashing at the weeds in front, followed the white banners that were fluttering in the wind invoking the spirit of the dead, and trod lazily and listlessly up the hills, and across a stretch of rape fields, trampling the soil, leaving behind a trail of footprints. The trail grew longer and longer. Finally a long and winding path was visible ....

Had the earthquake been caused by the heavy footsteps of people trampling on the soil?

I shouted at the top of my lungs, but there was no response from the houses and shops on either side of the street. Only a dim yellow light went on in a building in the distance. Was it the school or the town hall?

Earthquake! An earthquake! — It took me a long while to realize that there was no sound coming from my vocal cords. I pinched my hand to see if I was dreaming.

I was overcome with anxiety. The rustling sound was growing louder, and troops of rats were scurrying out from under the doors, from their hiding holes in the trees, from narrow alleys, from vegetable fields and even from the other side of the slope. They were all fleeing in my direction. The entire street was teeming with rats. They came in waves, ebbing and flowing, rising and falling, spreading all the way to the foundations of the walls and the foot of the pillars. It was impossible to step aside to avoid them. I was treading on rats — soft, slippery — like treading on a cotton wool mattress, or on a pile of driftwood in the river. No matter how I leapt and picked my way, I couldn't land on solid ground.

The even stranger thing was, the rats didn't make a sound, nor did they mind me no matter how hard I stamped on them. They just scrambled out from under my shoes and then pushed on. The most they would do was to scamper blindly up to my waist and shoulders, and then they would leap to the ground again to join the other escapees. They pressed on, shoulder to shoulder, treading hard on each other's heels, showing a solemn and whole-hearted commitment to a plan and a conviction that you had no way of knowing.

I moved unsteadily on the surface of the water of this rat-river, ran half-stumbling for a while, walked half-stumbling for a while, and then ran again, and then walked again, knocking on every door I went past. Earth — quake —!

The rat-tide cascaded over a flight of steps, it came rolling down like balls, like tubes which broke open when they hit the bottom of the street, and you could see their grey underbellies. The alley at the crossroads ahead was narrow, and the rat-tide rose all of a sudden, knocking down a meat-stand. A urine-bucket also went swirling for a while before it toppled and was swept away by the rat-tide.

Firecrackers were still exploding. The children were squeezing their way through the crowd looking for the remains of firecrackers that had gone off. The women, supporting one another or leaning against one another, were watching with apprehension and bewilderment the pomp and ceremony accorded a person after her death. Some found it a great pity that the deceased had no one to carry on the family line, others remarked that she had three neph-

ews but only one turned up, and what about his wife? And did the
one who turned up cry or not? He did. A lot? Well, not really, he
seemed ....

The rest of what they said was lost on me. My body was parched
and stiff, and I could find nothing to say. All I could do was thank
people for their tears, thank the deputy-mayor of the town, the
village chief, the elderly, the women and the children, thank the
young woman who, for reasons which escaped me, had sobbed a lot
harder than the rest and had tried to disappear into the crowd ....
I thanked them all — people whose faces were unfamiliar to me
and whose eyes were red from crying. And, to express my gratitude
for the company they provided for her on this first leg of her
homeward journey, I went down on my knees.

White rice was scattered into the air, handfuls and handfuls of
it. Grains of rice fell into the grave, bounced once or twice, and then
lay still. The distant mountains became blurred and their outlines
soft, rock piles heaped upon one another at an oblique angle began
to rise and fall, rise and fall. It was as if sheets of roaring waves, long
frozen, were melting into blue surging waters again, and there
would be a re-enactment of the ancient mythical story of the flood
that drowned the whole earth. All sound had been made transpar-
ent by the heat of the sun and had turned into soundless grains of
salt flickering and shimmering on the raging billows.

I tried desperately to cry, but I couldn't. I couldn't think of a
single past event related to Aunt Yao that could move me to tears.
I could only remember her furtive giggle. Heavens! What was she
giggling about?

I dashed here and there on the rat-tide hoping for a break-
through. The milky white river ahead exuded a freshness that was
damp and chilly, giving rise to masses of misty vapour. The rat-tide,
strong as ever, was cascading over the street and streaming towards
the river, I had no idea what was calling them, summoning them to
the other shore. The rats in front had sunk, but those at the back

trampled on them and pressed on. They, too, sank, but those behind fought on fearlessly. When they tumbled into the water, they got drenched, and tried desperately to scramble to the shore. Many bit one another's tails to get their bearings, often five or six of them in a row, and they flopped about in the water like a black whip, throwing up clouds of spray. Splash! Splash! The sound was like the cheers that broke out in a certain square. It could, I believe, even erode the cliffs.

The rat-tide was like a long black blanket and the waves rolled effortlessly upon it, crushing it. But the tossing waters covered an ever-larger area until it took the shape of a long tongue licking its way across the river towards the opposite shore. It came upon a boat half way down the river, and all at once the roof of the boat, its side and the oars were taken over by the rats. The boat became a rat-island.

No, it wasn't a rat-island. It wasn't. I saw clearly, it was the rush basket filled with charcoal slags that was standing in a corner by the door in my house. It was Aunt Yao's basket.

> The mountains oh, the bones of our forebear, Pan Gu!
> The rolling hills oh, the body of our forebear, Pan Gu!
> His eyes — ah, the sun and the moon!
> His teeth — ah, gold and silver!
> His hair — ah, plants and trees!
> And since then, ah, birds and animals appeared in the land!

The song master intoned and everyone started to sing. The earth was shaking, the cliffs were crumbling. The Book of Heaven had unfolded, the bows were drawn taut. Severed buffalo heads, dripping blood, hung beneath battle standards of warring tribes. Where would you go? Brother marries sister, an ancient world-legend covering the earth like ferns before all time — bitter, tenacious had woken up every dream in the black hole of Time, in deserts, in primeval forests, in palaces draped in green mottled moonlight, where am I? A momentous ejaculation in ancient times, and a shrill scream during labour, had torn the boundaries of earth and heaven, forcing the blood of mythical emperors Yan and Huangdi into the very foundations, into sunless coal seams, into hieroglyphics that arrived furtively, in conspiratory tangled whispers, and into the slashed throats and rattling shackles of condemned rebels in prison cells, where would you go? Oh! Oh! The deluge, the deluge! One person has died, the earth is shaking, the walls are crumbling, no one could save her just as none could turn the boundless universe inside your heart and mine into mere inventory. In the end, the sun is still out of reach; the meteor descends only in paint; an-eye-for-an-eye, murmurs, whispers — they are ephemeral. And yet, year after year, Time reveals eternity and the perfect harmony of the *taichi* in the ears of grain — to what end? Death is woven with death to bear witness to the immortality of the human race, to point towards the jade trees and jewelled palaces in heaven, the fragrant blossoms and lush vegetation, mountains of grain, seas of cotton, the phoenixes that bless matrimony, and the arrival of good men and women amidst waves of joyous singing, their hands joined, their long flowing sleeves entwined, their faces like peach-blossoms. Oh, this glory that is incomparably real where would you go? There have always been plateaus. There have always been constellations and caves. There have always been swords and halberds that clashed, and empty boats in desolate waters. There have always been children with tearless eyes, barren women with their vain mirrors and streams of people like ants where would you go? Walls have crumbled, the earth is shaking. But even if every leaf of the calendar marks the anniversary of the death of thousands of people, even if every road is endless, even if repression and indulgence will change in manifestation, do we not, for these reasons, find the bitter answers seeping out from the rocks ever so sweet? Do we not consider ourselves fortunate to have been born and bred in this land, fortunate that memories cascading over us like an avalanche and ideals fierce and untamable, will never again leave us, never, and will bring salvation to each self? Tombstones, crumbling and dilapidated, bear vivid testimony to the good men and women who proclaim in silence maxims true for all time : every act of sowing is a harvest and not a harvest every kind of beginning is a repetition and not a repetition real or genuine death has always existed and has never existed in humans in animals in lightning thunder ice and frost in metal wood water fire and earth the deep rumbling voices of man overgrown with moss where would you go Lao Hei where would you go where ...?

His breath had become the wind and his perspiration —
    ah, the rain!
His blood had become rivers and there will be,
    ah, eternal spring!
People were still singing, singing.

Finally the quake came. Afterwards, they said that the ancient border wall had collapsed, leaving not a single trace. I went to have a look. It was true.

8

Lao Hei had just taken a bath. Her hair was wet, and the warmth exuding from her pores rose from her collar. She lay curled up in bed like a well-behaved kitten, her pointed chin resting on her palm. When she turned her head to one side, the side where the curtain was, a vein stood out tube-like below her earlobe, like a bayonet holding up the white flag, making her look fragile and beautiful. She knew it, of course. She swung her long slim legs round into an even more provocative posture. Then she smiled enigmatically, "When you handed me the soap just now, didn't it occur to you to open the door a bit wider?" I nearly burst out laughing, but I checked myself, lest she couldn't take it, "Those culottes you're wearing, they're no longer in fashion now." She retorted with a sneer, "Loyal Supporter of the Revolution, don't you think you've led a miserable life?" I threw her a cigarette, and stuck one between my teeth, "You don't have much time left."

It was true, she didn't have much time left. Her hair was turning grey, and her face was wrinkled, like parched soil. I thought about how she liked to perform *qigong* exercises before her admirers, not always successfully, and I had the feeling she'd look pretty much like a witch in the dim light. Why was she so crazy about shopping, munching snacks as she went? Why did she like to play the fool, the helpless child, the coquette, the philosopher and the bitch before men and yet never let slip the opportunity to smile charmingly to them? Calculated smiles lead to all sorts of problems, and it was only natural that there should already be lines on her face. Besides, everyone knew that that dainty mouth of hers with its sweet smile opened onto a pair of lungs ravaged by cigarettes, and insides that reeked of half-digested or undigested titbits.

How pathetic! Everybody grows old. You can't win all the time. And even if you did, so what? Once, muttering to herself, she let slip the remark, "Damn! Men all say the same things as soon as the door is closed. How weird!" She was then polishing her shoes, and she stared at the toes and smiled wanly.

She had rung me up and asked me to come over probably because she wanted me to fill the growing emptiness around her. She must have realized that my sofa was grotty, that my wife was away because of a lawsuit to do with reforms and I was completely worn out and would be too weak to protect myself. If that really was the case, she was even more pathetic. For I just wiped a hand over my face, gently patted the arm of her sofa and said, "Time I went. I got things to do."

When men tried to shake her off, kindly or maliciously, they probably all said the same thing, and their excuses were equally lame.

"Go then!" She tossed her head indifferently. But after a while, she mumbled something about how she ought to go and get some instant noodles. She didn't have to invent such an excuse, actually. I wouldn't think any the worse of her if she saw me off part of the way. She should just do what she wanted to do, there was no need to rack her brains wondering what to say and how to act before me.

"What a nice day," I said.

"Those fucking sleeping pills," she muttered.

"You dream a lot at night?"

"It's that rapping noise underneath my bed."

"Haven't you found out what it is?"

"Maybe it's nothing."

"Perhaps you ought to go back to the factory and be a lab assistant, or go and set up a farm, like the one we set up when we were sent down to the countryside."

"Forget it. I've seen through everything long ago."

"You haven't seen through the meaning of seeing through."

"I told you before. Don't give me that crap about meaning and responsibility and what not! It's damn ridiculous!"

"I've told you before, too. You've all the time been riding high on other people's sense of responsibility and meaning and what not. Damn, it's not ridiculous!"

Outside, the sun was so strong I narrowed my eyes. When I turned round to look at her, I suddenly felt that she seemed much smaller than she was inside. And the more I looked at her, the more I felt that there was something strange about her pallid skin and her puffy eyelids — she, too, looked like a fish!

I said goodbye and left. The sharp, pointed shoulder blades under her clothes gradually receded into the bustling crowd. Her figure shrunk to a black speck, like a lump of sugar that was dissolving in water.

I stamped on the accelerator of my motor bike and saw in the rear mirror one fast-moving lorry after another, while the display shop windows on either side of the street reflected a continuous stream of traffic. I felt as if I was in a big, noisy, busy square. Rows of tall buildings were waiting to be finished, it looked as though they were struggling to emerge from a chrysalis of scaffolding and safety net to soar into the sky upon their beautiful wings. The main bridge, like a bow drawn taut, made me a little nervous as I zoomed up to the top, towards the blue sky. I was worried that all at once the arrow would be let loose and the bow left quivering, rocketing me into outer space. In the meantime, tons of golden sunlight was rushing out of the open door of that red-hot oven to come splashing down to this city — this noisy bustle that was growing louder and louder.

I swept past a young man who, laughing and shouting, was pedalling a pedicab loaded with fruit and a young woman. His bulging muscles were so tanned and so beautifully flexed that I couldn't help but turn round to look at his face. I felt that this body, so full of life and vitality, was a good omen for me — perhaps I could speak more eloquently at the meeting this afternoon; or perhaps I would, after that turning at the junction ahead, meet a certain person, one whom I'd never met but had long been waiting for.

I was getting nearer and nearer the junction.

What would I see? What had I been waiting for?

In the end, I didn't take the turning and I didn't backtrack, I just drove on. I didn't have much time. When I got home, I'd get something to eat, then I'd do the dishes, then I'd ring Yuan for an appointment. Maybe we still wouldn't agree on anything, but I had to keep talking, for the sake of this city, for the sake of the person on the other side of the junction whom I hadn't seen just now.

There really was no point thinking too much about things. The days had to be spent like this, should be spent like this — after you've eaten, you do the dishes; when you've done the dishes, you make a phone call .... Get that and you've got the simplest and most profound truth about life. I remembered that Aunt Yao had mumbled something about a bowl of yam before she died, as if she was trying to come to grips with some knotty problem. For a long time, her words had made me feel as though there was a block in my mind. But now, I'd finally seen the light; I'd found the answer:

When you've eaten, you do the dishes.

That's all.

Xu.[6]

January 1986

---

[6] According to the author, there are two schools of explanation for the word "xu". One is that it was used in ancient times as a term of address by the people of Hunan and Hubei for their elder sisters. Another is that it was used in ancient times as a term of address by the people of Hunan and Hubei for all their female relatives. A more detailed explanation of this word in its second sense is provided by the author in the last paragraph of page 128.

Renditions Paperbacks

CURRENT FICTION TITLES:

Han Shaogong: *Homecoming and Other Stories*
trans. Martha Cheung   ISBN 962-7255-13-0

Liu Sola: *Blue Sky Green Sea and Other Stories*
trans. Martha Cheung   ISBN 962-7255-12-2

Liu Xinwu: *Black Walls and Other Stories*
ed. Don J. Cohn   ISBN 962-7255-06-8

Mo Yan: *Explosions and Other Stories*
ed. Janice Wickeri   ISBN 962-7255-10-5

Tao Yang: *Borrowed Tongue*   ISBN 962-201-381-3

Wang Anyi: *Love in a Small Town*
trans. Eva Hung   ISBN 962-7255-03-3

Wang Anyi: *Love on a Barren Mountain*
trans. Eva Hung   ISBN 962-7255-09-2

Xi Xi: *My City: a hongkong story*
trans. Eva Hung   ISBN 962-7255-11-4

Xi Xi: *A Girl Like Me and Other Stories*
trans. Rachael May & Chu Chiyu   ISBN 962-201-382-1

Yu Luojin: *A Chinese Winter's Tale*   ISBN 962-201-383-X

Contemporary Women Writers: Hong Kong and Taiwan
ed. Eva Hung   ISBN 962-7255-08-4

Orders and enquiries to:
Renditions, Chinese University of Hong Kong, Shatin, NT., Hong Kong
Telephone (852) 2609-7407   Fax (852) 2603-5149